"I don't need a baby-sitter!"

Elliott said in frustration. "I'm a thirty-two-year old man."

"You're just a babe in the woods," Mallory argued. "You've got to force yourself to be less the stereotypical absentminded scientist. After all, brown socks with a navy suit and black shoes don't cut it." She smiled when he automatically glanced down, then flushed in annoyance.

"As for your social life," she went on, "I'm going to introduce you to my friends and teach you to mingle with normal people. Then we're going dancing."

Elliott stared at her thoughtfully, and she blushed at her own presumptuousness. "Don't you think my plan is a good one?" she asked with less confidence.

"I think it's excellent, and I have an idea that should prove the pièce de résistance."

He was smiling broadly. Something about that smile and the way he was looking at her made Mallory a bit wary. "Just what *is* this idea of yours? I said I'd teach you to make small talk and dance, but I didn't say anything about—"

"Lovers," Elliott supplied. "I want you to become my lover, Mallory Littlefield...."

Gina Wilkins will likely never forget the months spent working on *A Stroke of Genius*. She was pregnant with her third child, and childbirth came right on the heels of completing the last manuscript page! So double congratulations are in order—to the Wilkins family of Jacksonville, Arkansas, on the arrival of the beautiful baby David, and to Gina, for her sixth wonderful Temptation.

Books by Gina Wilkins

A Stroke of Genius

GINA WILKINS

Harlequin Books

TORONTO • NEW YORK • LONDON
AMSTERDAM • PARIS • SYDNEY • HAMBURG
STOCKHOLM • ATHENS • TOKYO • MILAN

FORTY YEARS OF
Romance

Published August 1989

ISBN 0-373-25362-1

1

ELLIOTT'S SISTER would have called the look on his face "sulky"—despite the number of times he'd retorted that geniuses did not sulk. They withdrew, they had moods and tantrums, they were sometimes forgetful or thoughtless. They didn't sulk.

Sybil had never believed him.

Okay, he thought in glum resignation, hunching lower in the back seat of the cab. So maybe he was sulking. But, dammit, he didn't know what to do, and for Elliott Fraser, not knowing what to do was a rare occurrence. Very rare.

And then his unhappy gaze fell onto a brightly colored sign on a building that the cab was just passing. Lone Star Employment Agency. "Stop the cab!" he demanded impulsively, leaning forward to catch the driver's attention. "I want to go into that office!"

MALLORY HAD NO TROUBLE at all with the application until she came to the section asking her to list all the jobs she'd held for the past five years. There were two problems with that part—remembering all the jobs and then finding space to list them in the page and a half she'd been allotted for that purpose. She gulped, took a firmer grip on the pencil, shifted the clipboard on her knee and grimly began with the job she'd just left, as requested in the instructions.

"Employer—Gladwell's Insurance Agency," she muttered beneath her breath, filling in the blank and ignoring the four other women completing identical applications in the chrome and vinyl reception area of the employment agency. "Position—office manager. Salary—not nearly enough," she stated flatly, though she wrote the proper numbers on the line provided. "Reason for leaving—"

There she paused. Looking up with a frown, she unintentionally caught the eye of the attractive black woman sitting beside her, forging through her own application. "How do you explain that you left your last job because the boss was an arrogant, obnoxious male chauvinist who demanded perfection from others without ever acknowledging his own incompetence?" Mallory asked the woman whimsically.

"Personality conflict," the woman replied without hesitation before looking back down at her own form.

"Oh, that's a good one." Mallory scrawled the two words onto the appropriate blank and looked at them approvingly. Yeah, she liked that. Liked it so well, in fact, that she used the same explanation for the next four jobs she listed. "Personality conflict covers a lot of area," she murmured with a rueful smile. It wasn't that she was hard to get along with. It was just that she—well, her mother always said Mallory marched to a very odd drummer. She'd tried to conform, she really had, she told herself self-righteously. It was just that something always went wrong. And still she continued to hope that the next job would be exactly what she'd been looking for in her restless pursuit of personal fulfillment—a goal that had been frustratingly elusive through most of her twenty-six years.

She and all the others in the room were startled when the door to the office opened with a forceful crash. Mallory looked up at the man who'd entered and stood frowning sternly around him, seeming to study each of the five women who waited in the reception area. He was a handsome man, she thought in automatic approval, despite his rather disheveled and somewhat mismatched clothing. Early thirties, well over six feet tall, slightly mussed auburn hair, unusually dark skin tone for a redhead—and no freckles, she noted with the envy of a woman possessing the classic redhead's complexion.

His intense gaze settled on her, lingering for an uncomfortably long time. Finally he spoke. "Can you type?" he asked curtly.

Caught off guard, she nodded. "Well, yes—"

"Answer phones?"

"Of course, but—"

"Keep up with appointments, letters, that sort of thing?"

"Sure, but—"

"Are you married or engaged?"

She stared at him. "No."

"Okay, you'll do. Come on." He opened the door and motioned for her to precede him.

Startled into a breathless laugh, Mallory shook her head. "You can't be serious."

"Sir, may I help you?" the flustered receptionist asked, approaching with quick, nervous steps.

"This is an employment agency, isn't it?" he asked impatiently. "This woman's looking for a job, and I need an employee. I'm hiring her."

"But, sir, that's not the way we do things. You need to talk to a counselor—"

"Now, why should I do that?" the man asked in seemingly genuine confusion. "I've already found someone."

"This guy's nuts," the woman sitting next to Mallory muttered. "He really thinks you're just going to walk out of here with him."

"But you don't even know what type of job this woman is looking for!" the receptionist protested bravely.

The man was beginning to look harried. Focusing his dark brown eyes on Mallory, he tilted his head in inquiry. "You're not a brain surgeon, are you?"

"I'm a secretary," she admitted, unable to look away from the appeal in those beautiful eyes.

His smile made her gulp for breath. "Great. I'm an independent businessman who just happens to be in need of a secretary. Will you work for me?"

Everyone in the room turned toward Mallory, waiting for her reply. She flushed at the attention, knowing they were all expecting her to tell the maniac to get lost. Which, of course, any rational, practical, normal type of secretary would do. Mallory could almost hear the drumroll of her dear, odd drummer. "Maybe you'd better look at this," she said, thrusting out the nearly completed application.

It took him about two minutes to read the entire application. Then he glanced up with a grin. "You and I," he told her in approval, "are going to get along just fine."

"Sir, I'm going to have to insist—"

Ignoring the receptionist, the man continued to look at Mallory. "Well?"

"I'm going to want more money than I made on the last job," she warned him. Something told her she'd earn it.

He waved his hand in a negligent gesture. "Fine. Now could we go? I'd like you to start right away."

The woman sitting beside Mallory caught her arm as she started to rise. "Honey, you can't just go off with this guy. He's obviously crazy."

Mallory picked up her purse, gently shrugging out of the woman's grasp. She wasn't sure who the crazy one was just then, but she suspected it was herself. "I'll be okay."

"But you can't *do* this," the receptionist wailed, wringing her hands. "Our fee!"

"Bill me," Mallory's new employer suggested, ushering Mallory out the door.

"But I don't know who you are!" The protest faded behind them as Mallory and her mysterious boss started down the hallway.

"Come to think of it, *I* don't know who you are," Mallory remarked as they stepped through the exterior doors to the parking lot. "What's your name?"

"Elliott."

"First or last?"

"First. Elliott Fraser." He looked expectantly around the parking lot. "Do you have a car? I sent my cab away."

She swallowed. She'd expected to follow him in her car as he drove his own, giving her a chance to have a long, stern talk with herself about her impulsiveness and perhaps to change her mind about accepting this job. "Yes, I have a car."

"Which one?"

She nodded to their right. "The blue Ford."

Elliott frowned. "You *do* need a raise, don't you?"

"Pay me enough to buy a Porsche, and I'll even make an effort to be on time to work in the mornings," Mallory replied flippantly.

"Forget it."

She grinned as she settled behind the wheel, watching him fold his long legs into the passenger side of the compact car. "Well, it was worth a shot. Mind if I ask where we're going, Mr. Fraser?"

"Elliott. And we're going to my office."

"Our office," she corrected. "I'm working for you now, remember?"

"Yeah, right."

She started the car, then sat staring thoughtfully out the window until her passenger stirred restlessly beside her. "Elliott?"

"Yes?"

"Don't you think this is a little weird?"

He looked surprised. "What?"

"I mean, the way you hired me and everything. God knows I think it's weird, and things like this happen to me all the time. You'd think I'd be used to them by now. But even *I* never did anything quite this strange before."

Elliott shook his head in a gesture of impatience, causing the summer sunlight to glint off the coppery highlights in his dark red hair. "I don't see what the big deal is. You need a job and I have one. I think we went about it in a very efficient manner, without wasting anyone's time."

She twisted in her seat until she was facing him. "Just answer one question, okay?"

He nodded.

"You're not into anything illegal, are you?"

He stared blankly at her. "Of course not. What in the world makes you ask that?"

"Experience," she replied with a sigh, finally putting the car into reverse. "Tell me how to get to our office."

Elliott gave the directions, then sat back to watch her as she drove. She handled the little car very well, he noted in approval. He hated being driven by incompetents, and there were entirely too many of those loose on the highways. Someday he was going to have to learn how to drive.

Mallory Littlefield. She didn't look like a Mallory Littlefield. She also didn't look twenty-six years old, but he'd read the application and had committed it to his photographic memory. If asked, he could have reeled off her address, her educational background, place of birth and all five of the former employers she'd listed. He didn't find it at all odd that she'd come with him. She'd been bored and annoyed with the application she'd been working on when he'd found her. He'd known the minute he saw her that she was the type who'd appreciate the straightforward, direct approach he took to such things.

Elliott wasn't one to dwell on another person's out-
ward appearance, but he enjoyed looking at Mallory.
She wasn't beautiful—not in the way Sybil was beautiful. But Mallory was interesting, he decided, studying her profile. Her face was sort of round, with a short,
straight nose dusted with golden freckles, a firm, stub-
born chin and a full, mobile mouth that seemed compelled to tilt upward into a smile. Her eyes, just visible
beneath the long, shaggy bangs she wore, were green,
uptilted at the corners and mirrored a lively, curious
intelligence. Her hair was cinnamon red, caught up into
a twisted ponytail at the top of her head which, com-
bined with the long bangs, gave her a rather appealing
Pekinese appearance. Sybil would probably call her
cute. She dressed a bit oddly—safari styling, lots of
loose khaki—but perhaps that was popular these days.
Elliott wasn't one to keep up with fashion.

"Mallory?"

"Mmm?"

"What do you mean by experience?"

She slanted him a questioning look. "I beg your pardon?"

"When I asked why you thought I might be involved
in something illegal, you said you were asking from experience."

"Oh. Well, it's simple, really. I took this job once that
was listed in the newspaper. The man was really nice,
very attractive, expensive clothes. It was a one-woman
office, he told me, mostly telephone work. I worked
there for two weeks thinking I was booking models for
photography sessions. Turned out I was making ap-

pointments for some really expensive call girls. I quit two days before the whole operation was busted."

"Oh."

It seemed to be her turn to speak again. "Why did you ask if I were married or engaged?"

Glancing at her new employer, she saw the look of discomfort that slid across his attractive face. "You may be working some long hours occasionally," he explained after a pause. "Husbands and fiancés tend to get in the way at such times."

"Oh."

They didn't speak again until Elliott pointed out the road Mallory was to turn onto. Expecting to find an office building, she found, instead, a large, two-story older home. The pale yellow frame structure was an odd mixture of Victorian and New England farmhouse with white shutters, mismatched gingerbread trim and a full-length front porch complete with a swing. Mallory fell in love with the house at first sight. "*This* is your office?"

"This is my home," he corrected. "My office is downstairs. Come on."

"Before we go in," she said, clearing her throat, "just what is it that you do, Elliott?"

He cocked his head and looked thoughtful, seeming to deliberate on his reply, making her wonder why the question had been at all difficult to answer. Finally he shrugged, gave her an appealing, slightly crooked grin and admitted, "I'm a genius."

"Of course you are," Mallory said very politely. "I should have spotted that right away. People pay you for that, do they?"

Elliott stared at her for just a moment before his grin widened. "Very good. Sounds like something Sybil would have said."

Sybil? Before she could ask, he went on, "Actually I'm paid for writing articles and textbooks, the occasional lecture or consulting job and for work I do with Option Forum, a think tank that operates out of California. We meet there once each quarter for several days at a time. Oh, and I'm also paid for inventing—mostly computer-related accessories—though I hate to limit myself to any one field of interest."

By this time Mallory was the one staring. "You really *are* a genius. What were you, one of those kids who graduated college at sixteen, had a doctorate by eighteen?"

"Well, actually, the doctorate came on my nineteenth birthday. My thesis was my first published textbook."

"And how old are you now?" she asked curiously.

"Thirty-two."

"Wow. I did well to finish high school and two years of secretarial college."

Elliott shrugged. "I'm helpless at secretarial skills. We all have our talents."

She smiled at him. "That was very nice, Elliott."

He winced and reached for the door handle. "You may not think I'm so nice after working for me for a few days. I'm not all that easy to work for. I've forgotten how many secretaries I've had, but they all quit after less than a month. Sybil's the only one who could work with me for any length of time."

Sybil, again. Mallory was still wondering who Sybil was as she followed Elliott into the house. The inside turned out to be as wonderful and eccentric as the outside. She could be perfectly happy living in such a place, she decided approvingly.

"This is your office," Elliott announced, opening a door with a rather formal flourish. "Mine is across the hall."

She'd expected chaos, though she couldn't have explained why. Instead, she found a fully equipped state-of-the-art office that was almost intimidatingly neat. "Your last secretary left fairly recently?" she guessed aloud.

Elliott nodded. "She left for a three-week cruise this morning."

Mallory whirled around to stare at him. "Three weeks! But I was under the impression you were offering me a permanent job, not a temporary one. Elliott, I need a real job."

"This *is* a real job," he assured her. "She won't be returning after the cruise. She's getting married and moving out of state—though she doesn't know it yet," he added beneath his breath.

Mallory wondered if she'd heard him correctly. "I beg your pardon?"

"Never mind." He motioned toward the desk. "Here's a list of everything that needs to be done immediately. I'll be in my office if you need me."

"I—uh—" She wasn't sure what she'd been about to ask, but it wouldn't have mattered. Elliott was gone. Sighing, Mallory turned back to the desk—*her* desk, she corrected herself—and stowed her roomy leather bag in a lower drawer. Elliott had been right about the list. His last secretary must have been a real stickler for organization, she thought, impressed as well as a bit daunted. How was she supposed to follow an act like this?

Gulping, she reached for a folder marked Bills To Be Paid by the Fifteenth. Today was the tenth; she might as well get that done. The so-helpful notepad gave specific directions for paying the bills, as well as describing where everything was.

Five minutes later Mallory stared at the numbers in front of her, then leaped to her feet. Quick, agitated steps took her across the hallway to the door Elliott had pointed out as his office. She knocked once and went in. The sight of his "office" almost made her forget why she'd crossed the hall. This was what she'd expected from his work area, she realized, looking slowly around the huge, impossibly cluttered room. It was stacked with computers, books, pieces of equipment whose use was foreign to her, papers and heaven only knew what else.

Elliott was bent over a computer in one corner of the room, heedless of the pile of reports balanced precariously on the shelf right above his head. He glanced up at her entrance. "Problem?"

She blinked, remembered why she'd come in and planted her hands on her hips. "Elliott, you're rich!"

He cocked one dark red brow, crossed his arms over his chest and leaned against a desk top. "Yes."

"No, I mean you're *really* rich," she said, waving her arms to illustrate. "Megabucks! Rolling in dough."

Looking at her with exaggerated patience, he tilted his head. "Is there any particular point you're trying to make here?"

She shoved her hands in the deep pockets of her bulky khaki skirt and shrugged, feeling suddenly embarrassed. "Well, no, I guess not. It's just that I was paying bills, and I couldn't help looking at the books and—you're so rich!" she added in a near wail. "And you expect *me* to keep your books and—and everything?"

He chuckled. "I have an accounting firm that handles most of my financial needs," he explained gently. "All you have to do is the day-to-day stuff—whatever that is. I'm sure it's all on the list."

"*Everything's* on that list," Mallory muttered. She would bet his last secretary hadn't completely lost her cool when confronted with Elliott's finances.

"Good. Then it shouldn't be so difficult for you to catch on." He straightened, still watching her curiously. "Haven't any of your former employers been well-off?" he asked, for lack of a better description.

"Well, sure," she replied. "It's just that most guys with that much money are such jerks. You're—well, you act so normal."

"For a rich genius," he clarified for her, grinning broadly now.

She groaned. "Okay, I've made a fool of myself—again. It just surprised me, that's all."

"You didn't make a fool of yourself," he assured her.

She grimaced, knowing he was trying to be nice, and wandered slowly around his office. "I suppose you know where everything is in here. You have your own system, right?"

Elliott winced. "Wrong. It's total chaos. I go into frantic fits several times daily because I've misplaced something vitally important in this wreckage. But if you ever attempt to organize in here, I may very well break your arm."

She laughed, undismayed by his teasing threat, and picked up a framed eight-by-ten photograph of nine men and three women. Elliott stood proudly in the center of the group. Mallory tried hard to suppress a giggle, but failed miserably.

"What's so funny?" Elliott demanded, still watching her closely.

"Nothing," she assured him, swallowing another giggle. Oh, Lord! She was going to be fired before her first day was over if she didn't get herself under control.

"Mallory," he said sternly, tilting her chin upward with one hand and frowning down at her. "Why were you laughing?"

She gave up. "I just took one look at that photograph and decided it looked like a convention of Nerds R Us—yourself excluded, of course. I'm sorry, it's just that everyone seems so serious, and so—well, out of it. I really didn't mean to make fun of your friends. These things just come out sometimes, and I can't seem to stop them."

"You can stop apologizing. I'm not going to fire you. That's a photograph of the members of the think tank I told you about. Sybil calls us the Geek Group. They're very nice people, but they're all the kind who have plastic pencil packs in their pockets, adhesive tape holding their glasses together and socks that don't match. It's a dirty job," he added with that attractively crooked grin, "but somebody's gotta do it."

Mallory looked up at him, vividly aware that his hand was still touching her jaw. She swallowed hard, acknowledging for the first time the attraction she'd felt for him from the moment he'd entered the employment office. This would never do, she told herself firmly. She'd tried a romance with an employer once, and it had been an abysmal mistake. She pulled away from his touch and stepped back. "You're making me feel very guilty. I should know better than to label others from appearance."

"I know you didn't mean anything by it, so don't feel guilty," Elliott assured her kindly. "I think your honest reactions are refreshing. Most people hide what they really feel behind polite prevarications. You say what you think."

"And I've gotten in more trouble for that," she muttered with a sigh. Her attention was caught by another framed photograph. There was no way this subject could be called a *nerd* or *geek* or any other derogatory term. The woman was quite simply beautiful. Auburn-haired, dark-eyed, classic features. Mallory told herself she didn't really hate her. "She's gorgeous," she said, her voice sounding hollow to her own ears. No wonder Elliott hadn't seemed particularly impressed by *her* odd charms, Mallory thought rather glumly.

"That's Sybil," Elliott told her, his voice warming and deepening in a way that told her he loved the woman very much.

Mallory fought off a ridiculous wave of depression. "Of course that's Sybil," she murmured. "Your—uh—wife?"

He looked surprised. "My sister," he corrected her. "She's the one who left on the cruise this morning. She's been working as my secretary for the past few years."

"And now she's going to be married." Mallory felt herself grinning like an idiot, but couldn't seem to help it. His sister! How nice.

"Well, if her boyfriend has anything to say about it, she will," Elliott qualified. "He intends to use this time to convince her."

"Marriage shy, is she?"

"Mmm," he murmured, nodding. "But she's very much in love with George. I think she'll marry him, once she's convinced she'll be doing the right thing."

"You and your sister are very close, aren't you?"

He nodded, his eyes suddenly hard to read. "Very. She's about the only person in the world I *am* close to. I don't—" He paused, shrugged and continued quietly, "I don't seem to interact very well with other people. Sybil says I'm completely lacking in all social skills."

"Obviously Sybil's not always right," Mallory refuted firmly. "You've interacted very well with me."

He cocked his head, seemingly intrigued by her statement. "You're right. I have." He smiled broadly. "How about that?"

Suddenly uncomfortable, Mallory swallowed and backed rather hastily away from him. "Well, I have work to do. See you later."

He was still smiling when she walked away. She wondered uneasily just why he suddenly looked so pleased with himself.

MALLORY'S FIRST DAY on the job had gone very well. She'd told Elliott good-night and left with the feeling that she'd finally found her niche—despite the unwelcome attraction to her boss that she was determined to ignore.

"He sounds . . . different," Mallory's mother, Jean, pronounced cautiously, after Mallory had told her parents the entire story over dinner at their house that evening.

"He sounds like a fruitcake," Mallory's father, Bill, said flatly. And then he smiled at Mallory, affection softening his weathered, usually stern features. "You and he should get along just fine."

Mallory made a face at him, then laughed reluctantly. "That's exactly what Elliott said when he read my job application."

"Kindred spirits," Bill murmured, reaching for another homemade roll.

"Hardly. He's a certified genius, rich as—well, rich—and I'm a normal, working-class person."

"Normal?"

Ignoring her father's teasing remark, Mallory pointedly turned to her mother. "At least now I can pay you back the money you loaned me this month."

"Don't hurry, darling. Pay us when you get everything caught up."

"And budget your salary this time," Bill cautioned. "Just because your boss is rich doesn't mean you will be. You've got to learn to—"

"Live within your means," Mallory finished in unison with her father.

"Disrespectful brat," he muttered darkly, though Mallory wasn't the least fooled by his tone. Her parents may not always have understood their only child, but they adored her, and Mallory was well aware of their love for her.

Celebrating her good luck in finding what she considered the perfect job, Mallory indulged herself in a second piece of her mother's chocolate pie before heading for her own tiny apartment, where she knew she'd sleep like a contented baby.

Not that babies ever had the kind of dreams she'd had during that night, Mallory admitted as she dressed for work the next morning. She only hoped she'd manage not to blush when she told her much-too-sexy boss good-morning.

2

BY THE END of her first full week of working for Elliott, Mallory discovered that the intimidatingly efficient Sybil had made one major error—she'd spoiled her brother quite badly. It was no wonder, Mallory fumed late Friday afternoon, that Elliott had never had any luck working with anyone else but Sybil. No one but an adoring sister would have put up with him.

She'd expected a certain amount of moodiness, even eccentricity from a man who made his living at being a genius. But the least he could have done was acknowledge that not everyone operated in the same ways he did. He began by reciting lists of things he wanted done—long lists. He invariably ended the instructions by demanding to know why the first items on the list she'd just jotted down hadn't been done yet. Mallory gritted her teeth and promised to get everything done as quickly as possible, even though she knew she'd be interrupted every fifteen minutes or so by him giving her another list.

As for taking dictation from him—well, they hadn't taught her about Elliott in secretarial college. He tended to ramble while dictating, interspersing sentences that weren't meant to be included, and she was supposed to know by osmosis which statements were and which weren't relevant. After she'd spent precious time assuring that the letter or report looked just right, he'd take a blue pencil and slash it to pieces, often making changes that made no difference whatsoever to the finished product. She quickly learned to do rough drafts— several times.

He wasn't at the office full-time. He spent several hours a week at the university where he served as a part-time instructor. When he was in the office, he either closeted himself for long hours in his work room or drove Mallory crazy with his frantic orders.

Answering the telephone—usually the easiest part of her job—became a grim test of her patience and tact. Some callers were never to be transferred to him—unless he just happened to be in the mood to talk to them that day, which she only found out *after* she'd skillfully averted the caller. He proclaimed others to be close friends who were never to be denied access to him, and then he'd yell at her for interrupting his latest important project with a call from one of those "close friends."

She had just finished typing a lengthy, involved report—her fourth typing of this particular project— when Elliott burst into her office, his hair standing dramatically at all angles, and demanded, "Where's the AmStar file?"

Mallory took a deep breath. "What AmStar file?"

"*The* AmStar file!" he answered impatiently, cheeks growing redder. "Where is it?"

"Elliott, I've never even heard of AmStar. I'm relatively new here, remember?" she returned with forced sweetness. "But if you'll give me a clue, I'd be happy to help you look for it. Did you check the filing cabinets in your office?"

"Of course I did! Look in yours."

"Yes, sir." Obediently, Mallory stood and flipped through the A drawer of her filing cabinet. No Am-Star. "I'm sorry. It's not here. Can you think of any other name it could be filed under?"

"AmStar! AmStar!" Elliott raved, waving his arms. "Where else could you have put it?"

"I didn't put it anywhere," Mallory protested, her temper fraying. "This isn't a name I've dealt with yet. I'd remember. Let's go look in your office. Maybe it's in one of those stacks in there."

"It's not in my office. Look on your desk."

Mallory counted to ten. "Elliott," she said finally, "*you* look at my desk."

They turned together to find the desk in question neatly cleared. It was close to the end of the work day, and the only thing on the desk was the report Mallory had just finished typing. "Do you see any files there?" she asked.

Elliott turned on one heel and stormed out of the room.

"Pig," Mallory muttered under her breath, as she reluctantly followed him. She found Elliott making even a worse mess than usual in his office, haphazardly slinging things all around him as he searched wildly for the missing file. On a hunch, Mallory opened the A drawer of his filing cabinet and scanned through the files there. A moment later she closed her eyes, counted to ten *twice*, then cleared her throat and spoke. "Elliott."

"*What?*"

She held up a manila folder. "What is this?"

He stared suspiciously at it. "That's the AmStar file. Where was it?"

"Under A in your filing cabinet. It was out of order, but if you'd checked three folders back, you'd have found it."

He shoved a hand through his already disarrayed hair, looked a bit sheepish for a moment, then recovered his usual arrogance. "You should be more careful when you're filing. My time is too valuable to waste looking for a misfiled folder."

That did it. Mallory very coolly and quite deliberately threw the file at his head. Then she turned, just as coolly and just as deliberately, and left him staring after her as she stamped across the hall to her own office.

"What the hell?" Elliott blocked the door of her office as she tried to leave, purse held firmly under her arm. "Why did you throw that file? You scattered papers everywhere. I insist that you pick them up and organize them as I had them originally."

"You," she informed him, "can take that file and shove it. And don't bother firing me," she added furiously. "I quit!"

He looked as stunned as if the filing cabinet had just exploded in front of him. "You what? Why?"

"I'd rather work for Attila the Hun! You have the manners of a gorilla, the finesse of a charging rhinoceros. You have no consideration for the feelings of others, no appreciation for anything anyone does for you. You treat me like one of your computers, expect me to read your mind half the time—well, I'm fed up with it! Maybe Sybil was the perfect secretary. Good for her.

Evidently I'm not. So goodbye, Elliott. You may send my check to my home address."

Elliott didn't move as Mallory approached, his tall, lean body efficiently blocking her exit. "Move it, Fraser," she advised through clenched teeth.

"Have dinner with me tonight."

Mallory couldn't believe she'd heard him correctly. She stopped abruptly, staring up at him. "Do what?"

"I asked you to have dinner with me tonight. Give me a chance to apologize and maybe to explain a little."

"Explain about what?" Mallory asked warily.

"A lot of things." When she didn't immediately respond, Elliott added, "Please." It was the first time he'd said that particular word all week.

Mallory sighed. She'd never been able to hold on to her temper for very long and, besides, there was still something about Elliott that got to her, regardless of her anger with him. "Okay, I'll have dinner with you. But no promises about whether I'll ever work for you again," she warned.

He ignored the warning. "I'll pick you up at seven, all right?"

"Fine." She motioned for him to step out of her way, and he did.

"Idiot," she muttered as she slammed her car door and started her engine. But this time she was talking about herself.

"SHE CAN'T QUIT," Elliott muttered, kneeling to gather the papers that had only recently been neatly organized in the AmStar file. "She'll ruin everything if she quits."

It had taken him nearly a week to finalize his plans for convincing Sybil that he was perfectly fine without her. But the plan hinged on Mallory. And if she quit . . .

Somehow he'd thought Mallory would last longer than the others. Turned out, instead, that she held the record for the shortest term of employment for him. And none of the others had quit quite so dramatically. Staring thoughtfully at nothing, he wasted a moment remembering how spectacular she'd looked in full temper. Her green eyes had sparked, her chin lifted regally. Oddly enough, his first impulse had been to kiss her until she'd forgotten why she was angry with him. Not exactly a normal Elliott Fraser action. But then, Mallory wasn't like anyone else he'd ever met. She made him feel things that he wasn't accustomed to feeling. And, he had to admit, those feelings, or the discomfort that had accompanied them, had caused him to react defensively, to be even more difficult to work for than usual. So much so that he'd actually forced her to quit.

She couldn't quit.

Their meeting that evening had to be handled very carefully, he decided, wishing rather wistfully for one of the more logical, less emotional problems he'd confront in an Option Forum session.

ELLIOTT WAS TEN MINUTES LATE picking her up. Mallory didn't mention it. Though she'd told herself she was being foolish, she'd taken particular pains with her clothing, wearing a slim-fitting peach silk dress that, though not her usual casual style, was quite flattering. It had been a gift from her mother. Elliott wore a dark blue suit with a white shirt, muted striped tie and black belt and shoes. Mallory didn't bother to point out that his socks were brown.

"You look very nice," Elliott told her, visibly uncomfortable in this social situation that was beginning to feel suspiciously like a date to Mallory. Hadn't she told herself she wasn't going to date Elliott?

"Thank you. Do you want to talk first or eat first?" she asked, her own uncharacteristic nervousness making her less tactful than usual.

He blinked. "I thought we'd combine them. Talk over dinner."

"Oh. Fine. Then I'm ready."

"Good. The meter's still running on the cab."

Freezing in the act of locking her door behind them, Mallory stared up at him. "The cab?"

"Yes. It's waiting in the parking lot," he explained.

"Elliott, do you always take cabs?"

He muttered an explanation that she didn't understand. She asked him to repeat it. Rolling his eyes, he shrugged defensively and blurted, "I can't drive, all right? I thought you already knew that."

"No, as a matter of fact, I didn't," she answered coolly, hiding her surprise at his revelation. A thirty-two-year-old man in Dallas who didn't drive? She wouldn't have believed it possible. "Send the cab away, Elliott. We'll take my car."

Guiding her car in the direction of the restaurant where Elliott had made reservations, Mallory finally couldn't restrain herself any longer. "Elliott, *why* don't you know how to drive?"

A sideways glance showed his cheeks to be suspiciously red when he answered. "I grew up in Chicago.

Our parents died when Sybil was just an infant and I was three, and we were raised by our grandparents, who were quite wealthy. Grandad never went anywhere without his driver, who also had the responsibility of taking Sybil and me wherever we needed to go.

"After it was acknowledged that I was special, in some ways, my grandparents treated me pretty much like royalty. I was encouraged to develop my capabilities to their maximum potential, discouraged from wasting valuable time on frivolous pursuits. Sports, social events, even driving. Grandad wanted me to use the time spent in transit studying in the back of the limo. After I finally moved out on my own, I did try once to learn to drive, but I was lousy at it, and I hate doing anything that I don't do well."

Mallory found his explanation incredibly sad. "Elliott, that's terrible."

"That I can't drive?"

"No—that you were denied a childhood! How old *were* you when your grandparents learned your IQ?"

"Five. But I had a good life, Mallory. My grandparents loved me and my sister very much, though they weren't always sure how to treat me, I guess. I think I intimidated them a bit. They were afraid they'd hold me back from what I could become."

"I don't care how bright a little boy is, he still needs to be allowed time to be a normal child," Mallory argued stubbornly. "I hope you'll keep that in mind if you have children and they inherit your intelligence."

"I never really thought of myself as a father," Elliott mused.

Keeping her eyes fixed on the road ahead, Mallory asked with assumed casualness, "Don't you ever intend to be married? Surely you've been in love a time or two."

"No, I've never been in love. There was a woman I was involved with for a while. She's a member of Option Forum, and we—um—saw each other when the group met, but that's been over for the past year. I think our relationship was a bit too cold even for a couple of socially-inept geniuses," he added, trying to end on a light note.

Mallory parked the Ford in a space close to the entrance of the restaurant, using the distraction of their arrival to change the topic of their conversation. She found it all too easy to imagine Elliott involved in a practical, uncomplicated, purely physical affair with another genius. The image twisted her heart.

Over dinner Elliott haltingly apologized to Mallory as he'd promised, for being so difficult to work for. He admitted that Sybil had carried on the tradition his grandparents had started of treating Elliott as someone very special, someone to be indulged and humored, handled with near awe. "I swear I've tried to get them all to stop treating me that way," he told Mallory, the sincerity in his expression making her believe in his frustration with the situation. "But the habit is a strong one, tough for any of us to change."

"Your grandparents are still living?" Mallory asked in surprise. For some reason, she'd thought they were dead.

He nodded. "Yes. They're in their seventies and still going strong. Still live just outside Chicago. I moved here about three years ago when the university offered me such a flexible association. Sybil joined me a year later when I admitted how much trouble I was having finding secretarial help."

Mallory toyed with her food for a moment, then set down her fork and gave up the pretense of eating, being so much more interested in her conversation with Elliott. "I think it will be good for you when Sybil marries and moves away, though I'm sure you'll miss her very much. It's not too late for you to start living a more normal life. I mean, you're obviously special, but you're human, Elliott. I respect you a great deal, but I'm not exactly in awe of you."

He grinned, the expression looking oddly boyish on his usually serious face. Mallory gulped in very feminine appreciation of his attractively sculpted features. "Something about the way you told me off this afternoon let me know that you weren't exactly in awe of me," he told her warmly, his dark eyes gleaming across the table at her. "Not many people would have done that. Sybil has occasionally cut me down to size, but she's the only one, really."

"You're sure you want a secretary who'll speak her mind and not one of those efficient, submissive types who'll never speak unless spoken to?" Mallory asked lightly.

"I want you."

She found herself suddenly trembling at his words, spoken in a deep, husky voice that seemed to glide right down her spine. Swallowing hard, Mallory reminded herself fiercely that Elliott meant he wanted her as his secretary. That was all. "Fine."

"Does this mean you retract your resignation?"

She nodded. "I told you I needed the job," she added offhandedly.

"Oh. Yes, of course."

She must have only imagined that there was the slightest trace of disappointment in his voice, because when she risked a quick glance at him she saw no evidence of that emotion—or any other—on his face. "Well," she said, deliberately brisk. "I'm glad that's settled."

"Yes, so am I." But rather than returning her tentative smile, Elliott frowned moodily down at his half-eaten dinner, seemingly lost in his own thoughts.

After a few moments of silence, Mallory cleared her throat to gain his attention. "Elliott?"

He blinked and looked up at her. "Yes?"

"Is something wrong?"

He sighed. "Yes."

"Is it about me? Are you worried that I won't be right for the job, after all?"

Immediately shaking his head, Elliott assured her he had no doubts she was exactly right for that position. Relieved, she relaxed, only then realizing how much she'd tensed at the thought that this dinner might, after all, be the last time she'd see him. "Would you like to talk about what's bothering you?" she asked hesitantly.

"It's Sybil," he admitted. "I'm afraid she's going to ruin her life because of me."

"What do you mean?"

He grimaced and pushed his plate aside. "George— the man she's been seeing—came to me on Monday morning, a few hours before he and Sybil left for their cruise. He told me that he's in love with her, and she with him, which didn't really surprise me. Then he told me that he'd asked her to marry him. She turned him down."

"She did? Why?"

Elliott ran a hand through his dark red hair, mussing it and making Mallory long to smooth it with her own hand. "George has been offered a promotion in his job that he'd be a fool to turn down. The problem is he'd have to move to Hawaii if he accepts it. Sybil doesn't want to leave Dallas because of me."

"Because she'd miss you?" Mallory couldn't imagine a woman turning down a man she loved to stay with her brother. True, she was an only child, but her friends with siblings wouldn't have hesitated to leave brothers or sisters to pursue their own lives. "Surely she knows that the two of you could stay close even if you lived in different parts of the country. There's always the phone and holiday visits."

"It's not that," Elliott denied, looking disgusted. "Sybil doesn't want to leave because she's thoroughly convinced that I would never survive on my own. She thinks I'm incapable of living in the real world without someone to shelter me from the harsh realities of everyday existence. She's also afraid I'll be lonely—that I need her to help me overcome my social deficiencies."

"You're kidding."

"I wish I were. But George leveled with me, telling me exactly the way Sybil feels. He was hoping I could convince her that she's being ridiculous to throw away her own chance of happiness because of an overdeveloped sense of responsibility to me."

"Didn't you say Sybil is younger than you are?"

Elliott nodded. "She's twenty-nine. But she's always been very—well, maternal toward me. She was always the practical one, taking care of the details I overlooked. As I said, it has become a very deeply ingrained habit."

Mallory shook her head, thinking in amazement of what he'd just told her. She knew what it was like to be different, of course. Her own parents often wondered aloud if she'd ever manage to find her own way in the world, ever learn to conform enough to fit in. But at least they knew she was capable of taking care of herself, one way or another. She wondered if Elliott's family took such smothering care of him because it kept them from being overly intimidated by his formidable intelligence. Perhaps they needed to know that he relied on them in some ways. And despite his half-hearted efforts to dissuade them, Elliott had fallen into the habit of allowing himself to be dependent on them. "I guess I can understand why Sybil would feel the way she does," she confessed.

Elliott's eyes widened. "Mallory, not you, too! Dammit, I'm a thirty-two-year-old man! I don't need a baby-sitter. I thought you, if no one else, would understand that."

"I do understand," she assured him, flattered by his inference that she saw him in a way that no one else did. "And I do believe that you're perfectly capable of taking care of yourself. But, Elliott, it's going to take a bit of effort for you to convince your family. Can you blame them for thinking you're helpless? You can't drive, you can't seem to work with anyone but Sybil on a full-time basis, you'd forget to eat half the time if your housekeeper or I didn't remind you. You lock yourself up in your workroom for hours, lost in that cerebral other world of yours, totally oblivious to whatever's going on around you. You're going to have to prove to your family that you *can* live like regular people."

He cocked his head in curiosity. "That's what I'd decided," he told her. "It was the reason I rushed out to hire another secretary right after Sybil left. I wanted her to see that I *could* work with someone else if I tried. And then I almost ruined it by being such a tyrant that I made you quit after only one week with me."

Fully drawn into the cause now, Mallory leaned her elbows on the table and shifted forward, ignoring the uniformed young man clearing their table. "It's going to take more than hiring a secretary, Elliott. You've got to work on those other areas, as well. I'd say learning to drive is your first priority. Prove you're capable of getting from place to place by yourself. Force yourself to be a bit less the stereotyped absentminded scientist—keep somewhat more regular hours, eat at normal mealtimes, don't wear brown socks with a navy suit and black shoes." She smiled when he automatically glanced beneath the table and then flushed in annoyance.

"As for your social life," she went on without pausing, "don't you have any friends in Dallas?"

He shrugged uncomfortably. "Not really," he admitted. "I have acquaintances, of course, but my real friends are scattered around the country. Most of them belong to Option Forum."

"It's wonderful that you have friends with so much in common, but you need more variety," Mallory pronounced firmly. "Lord, I've got friends who have nothing more in common with me than living in the same state. But we're still friends."

"I'll bet you have lots of friends," Elliott commented, unable to hide the hint of envy in his words.

"Dozens," she agreed cheerfully. "And I'm going to introduce you to them. Once you learn to mingle with normal people, maybe you can meet some all by yourself. I'm going to teach you to drive, too."

"Are you?" he asked dryly.

"Yep. Can you dance?"

He scowled. "Badly."

"Then we're going to dance. This is going to be great! How long do we have?"

"How long do we have until what?" he asked, looking a bit harried at the enthusiasm with which she was throwing out plans.

"Until you see Sybil again, of course. Until we have to demonstrate the changes you've made."

"Two weeks. When she and George return from the cruise, we're all gathering in Chicago for my grandparents' fiftieth anniversary celebration. I was hoping to convince her then that I want her to marry George and be happy—assuming, of course, that George doesn't succeed in convincing her during the cruise."

"That's not much time," Mallory mused thoughtfully. "But I think we can do it. A man with your brains oughta catch on quick enough," she added mischievously.

Elliott stared thoughtfully at her for a long time, until she finally blushed with the realization that she'd been presuming quite a bit by blithely making plans for him. "Don't you think my plan's a good one?" she asked with less confidence.

"I think it's excellent," he answered, rather to her surprise. "I've just had an idea that should prove the pièce de résistance. Added to the suggestions you've just made, my idea should convince Sybil once and for all that I no longer need her constant supervision to keep me from becoming lonely and maladjusted." He was smiling broadly when he finished, and something about that smile, and the way he was looking at her, made Mallory a bit wary.

"Just what is this idea of yours?" she asked.

"If Sybil thinks I've fallen in love, as she has with George, she'll realize that, not only would I no longer need her to keep an eye on me full-time, but that my sister's constant presence would actually be rather inconvenient. She could marry George with a clear conscience, knowing that I would have someone, too."

"You're going to tell Sybil you've fallen in love?" Mallory repeated slowly, her brows dipping downward. "With that woman you were involved with before—in your think tank?"

He shook his head firmly. "Oh, no. Sybil never approved of my relationship with Petra. She thought we were all wrong for each other, entirely too much alike. That our liaison was too cold, too passionless. She'd never believe I was in love with Petra."

"Elliott, I'm not sure she'd believe you if you made someone up. Sybil sounds pretty sharp, from what you've told me."

"Exactly," he agreed smugly. "Which means that I have to produce this woman for her examination. Have her with me at my grandparents' party."

Mallory twisted suddenly cold fingers in her lap. "You—uh—you have someone in mind, or were you planning to hire an actress for a weekend?"

"Oh, I don't think that will be necessary. I know just the woman who could pull this off." He winked at her.

"Now, Elliott—"

"You said you wanted to help me."

"Elliott, I said I'd teach you to drive and dance, introduce you to my friends. I didn't say anything about posing as your—as your—"

"Lover," he supplied for her. "I want you to be my lover, Mallory Littlefield. Will you go with me to Chicago?"

3

"ELLIOTT, this is the craziest plan I have ever heard. It will never work. I'll blow it—I know I will!" Mallory ranted as she followed him into his house. Since they were in her car, she'd offered to take him home rather than have him catch a cab from her place. He'd invited her in to continue the argument they'd begun at the restaurant. She'd been trying to convince Elliott since they'd left the restaurant that his idea of having her pose as his lover was absurd, but she might as well argue with her shoe. His mind seemed to be made up.

"You won't blow it, Mallory. And it's no crazier a plan than the one you came up with for me," he observed mildly.

"My plan had nothing to do with outright deception!" she protested indignantly. "I was just going to teach you a few necessary self-sufficiency skills. What you're asking me to do is to run a scam on your entire family."

"Run a scam?"

"You know, pull a fast one. Lie to them."

"Not such a terrible lie. Just think how good it will make them feel to believe that I'm not a lonely, frustrated man."

Mallory glared at him as he casually made himself comfortable on an overstuffed gray couch in the large downstairs living room. She'd never been upstairs. "Now you're making a play for my sympathy. It won't work, Elliott. I'm not quite as gullible as your family."

"Be honest, Mallory. Don't you think my idea is a good one?"

"I can see where it has its benefits," she admitted reluctantly. "I mean, if I were Sybil, I'd be relieved to know that you had someone who—but, Elliott, it's still not right."

"Let me worry about that part of it, will you? I've been responsible and logical and rational all my life. Isn't it about time I did something impulsive, maybe even a little foolish?"

Chewing her lower lip, she admitted silently that she thought it was past time for him to do something completely irrational, something that might even be rather fun in the long run. How many practical jokes had she played with her friends over the years? She doubted that Elliott had ever played a practical joke in his life. Not that this was a joke, exactly. He fully intended to convince his doting family that he was in love with her. With *her!* How absurd.

Still, she thought grudgingly, it wasn't as if anyone would be hurt by the deception. Just the opposite, in fact. Sybil would be reassured about her brother's well-being, his grandparents wouldn't worry about him being lonely, and they'd all start to see that he was quite capable of living in the "real world." When he decided the time was right—after Sybil was happily married, of course—he could casually announce that the relationship had ended quite amicably. Perhaps he'd even meet someone else to fill the position of his lover in reality. Her stomach clenched at that thought, but she ignored it. "You really think it would work?"

"It's a viable option," he pointed out with a faint smile, reminding her that he made a living coming up with ideas. Not usually such far-fetched ideas, of course, but workable ones. "I need you to help me with this, Mallory. Please."

Somehow he'd discovered that she just couldn't seem to resist him when he said "please" in that deep, slightly husky voice of his. Mallory sighed and gave in. "All right. But don't blame me if it all blows up in our faces."

His smile was almost blinding. "Great. When do we start?"

She frowned. "Start what?"

"Why, the instructions. You have to teach me to drive, to dance, to act like a lover."

"To do—what?"

"Mallory," he said with audible patience. "I've never been in love before. I don't know how to act like a man in love. If I'm going to convince my family, you're going to have to tell me what to do."

"Oh, I can't believe we're having this conversation," Mallory moaned, dropping into a striped armchair and covering her face with her hands. "Until I met you, I thought *I* was the strangest person I knew. Now I think I'm downright normal."

"So when do we start?"

She dropped her hands to look at him. "Your sister's in love. Just act like her boyfriend—George, wasn't it?—does around Sybil."

Elliott made a rueful face. "I really didn't pay much attention," he admitted. "I guess I've been so absorbed with my work lately—"

"What makes you think *I* know how a man in love acts?" she demanded.

He looked surprised that she'd even ask. "Well, I suppose you watch movies and read those romance novels women seem to like. And I assume you've been in love at some time—haven't you?"

"Well—"

He looked suddenly concerned. "You're not in love *now*, are you?"

"I told you there wasn't anyone special in my life the day you hired me," she reminded him. "And as for whether I've ever been in love—I thought I was once. But it was all a mistake, a real disaster."

He waved a dismissive hand. "Doesn't matter. I'm sure you'll know what I should do. Why don't we plan a driving lesson tomorrow? Maybe we can combine some of the lessons. We can talk about the way lovers act while we drive."

"My father always said I was going to end up in a real mess someday because of my impulsiveness," Mallory muttered. "Okay, we'll have our first lesson tomorrow. I'll pick you up after lunch."

"Great." He pushed himself to his feet when she stood. "You're leaving now? Wouldn't you like something to drink first?"

"No, I think I'll go on home. Something tells me I need to get plenty of rest tonight," she said with a sigh. "Good night, Elliott."

He caught her arm just as she reached the door. "You forgot something."

She tilted her head in question. "What?"

"Lesson one," he replied, just before he lowered his head to hers.

Mallory stood in frozen shock as Elliott's lips covered hers, his arms going around her to pull her close to his long, lean body. She certainly hadn't expected him to kiss her. She thought only for a moment of pulling away, but that sane impulse fled when he parted her lips with his tongue and deepened the kiss.

He kissed her a bit awkwardly at first, as if it had been a long time since he'd kissed anyone. But then something seemed to click, for both of them, and the embrace became explosive, urgent, both putting everything they had into it. Lips clinging, tongues entwining, bodies straining, hands exploring. When the kiss finally ended, Mallory found herself plastered against him, her arms around his neck, hands buried deep in his auburn hair, her breathing as ragged as his.

They simply stood that way for a long, silent moment, staring at each other as they tried to shake off the lingering effects of that devastating embrace. And then Mallory drew a deep, shaky breath and deliberately disentangled herself from him, stepping immediately back out of touching distance. She had to clear her throat before she could speak. "What was that for?"

His own voice was huskier than usual. "Practice. People in love, I believe, are quite fond of kissing each other."

"Well, yes, but I don't think it's necessary to practice quite so fervently. We can save the performances for your family gathering."

"What if I said it wasn't all a performance?" he asked her, watching closely for her reaction.

She clenched her hands behind her. "Elliott, don't make the mistake of thinking that there's anything real going on here. Remember it's all an act for your sister's benefit. I have a very strict rule against getting romantically involved with my employer."

"You're speaking from experience again?" he hazarded, though his expression changed little.

"Yes," she answered starkly.

"The time you thought you were in love—the mistake you told me about?"

"That's right. And I try never to make the same mistake twice."

He nodded thoughtfully. "I see."

She turned abruptly and reached for the doorknob. "Good night, Elliott."

"Good night, Mallory. I'll see you tomorrow."

She all but fled to the safety of her car. The effects of that kiss haunted her long into the night. By morning she was fully convinced that she was making one of the worst mistakes of her unconventional life.

ELLIOTT FOUND HIMSELF watching the clock impatiently on Saturday morning, wondering what time Mallory would arrive for his driving lesson. It had been a very long time since he'd looked forward to anything quite so much. Silly, of course. It was only a driving lesson and he dreaded the possibility of making a fool of himself once he got behind the wheel of a car. But he still found himself counting the minutes until he saw Mallory again.

Their kiss had been like nothing he'd ever experienced before. He'd kissed other women, of course, but the act had always been rather perfunctory—pleasant, certainly, but never so shattering. If merely kissing Mallory could have such an effect on him, he wondered what it would be like to actually go to bed with her. The thought made him warm with the beginnings of arousal even as it made him swallow in frustration. She certainly had no intention of going to bed with him, and he wasn't sure, himself, that he wanted their relationship to move in that direction.

He and Mallory had very little in common, actually. He'd never spent much time with women like her, and he would be willing to bet that she'd never gone out with a man quite like him. Yet, though he'd kissed Petra many times during their eighteen-month affair, none of their kisses had ever had the effect on him that Mallory's kiss had had. Just as he suspected that the sedate, rather clinical lovemaking he'd experienced with the other women he'd dated would have no comparison to making love with Mallory.

He'd be wiser to stick to women he understood somewhat better—women like Petra, who were no more impulsive, no more naturally passionate than he was. Perhaps that kiss with Mallory had simply been a fluke, a never-to-be-repeated eruption of pent-up emotions from a stressful week. If they were to kiss again, he'd probably find it no different from kissing

any other woman, no more magical than a touching of
lips, a meeting of bodies.

Pulling thoughtfully at his lower lip, he decided that
the practical, logical thing to do would be to conduct a
carefully controlled experiment and evaluate the results. Unfortunately there was nothing at all scientific
about his uncharacteristic anticipation of that particular experiment.

"PULL OVER! NOW!"

In obedience to Mallory's shouted command, Elliott
obligingly directed the car to the gravel shoulder of the
mercifully deserted country road she'd chosen for his
first driving lesson and turned off the engine. Then he
turned to look inquiringly at her. "What's wrong?"

"What's *wrong*?" she repeated in a near squeal. "Elliott, the first rule of driving is to keep your eyes on the
road. You missed that tree in the curve we just passed
by maybe half an inch. What were you looking at?"

"The tree. It seemed to have a fungal infestation that's
relatively rare in this part of the country. You usually
see such parasitic evidence only in—"

"I don't *care* what kind of fungus was in that tree,"
Mallory interrupted impatiently. "Elliott, *we* were almost in that tree. At forty-five miles an hour!"

"I told you I was a lousy driver," he muttered,
slumping behind the wheel. "Maybe I'd better stick to
cabs."

"There is nothing wrong with your driving," Mallory told him firmly. "You picked up the general han-
dling of the vehicle in an incredibly short time. I'm
amazed that you drive so smoothly on your first try in

who-knows-how-many years. Your only problem is concentration. When you're driving, you can't be thinking of your equations and observations or whatever else you usually think about. You have to think about your driving."

"Look at it this way," she went on when she saw that she had his full attention. "When you're driving, your own life is in your hands, but so are the lives of everyone you pass on the road and anyone who happens to be in the car with you. When I gave you the keys to my car and buckled myself into the passenger seat, I entrusted you with my safety. It's a big responsibility, but I happen to believe you're someone I can trust."

"Thank you," he told her unexpectedly, his expression grave as he looked steadily at her. "I consider that quite a compliment."

She hadn't meant for him to take her words quite so literally. She'd simply been trying to make a point about defensive driving, but something in his voice made her throat tighten. Why did he have to make everything so complicated? she wondered despairingly, resisting the urge to roll her eyes heavenward. "Look, we've been at this for nearly three hours," she said, glancing at her watch. "Are you hungry?"

"Yes."

"How does a picnic sound?"

He tilted his head in that characteristically curious manner of his that she found particularly endearing. "A picnic?"

"Sure. I just happened to pack one. I thought it would be fun."

"I haven't been on a picnic in . . ." He paused, rubbed his chin, then shrugged. "I'm not sure I've ever been on a picnic."

"Then you've definitely been missing something," she told him, fighting that tightening throat again. How easily he could disarm her! "Think you can concentrate long enough to drive about two more miles?"

He nodded gravely. "Yes. I won't betray your trust in me."

Managing not to sigh in exasperation, Mallory gave him directions to a little park just down the road, the one she'd had in mind when she'd impulsively packed the picnic supper.

"I think you're about ready to drive in traffic," she told Elliott as she spread the traditional red-and-white checked tablecloth beneath an enormous oak tree, ignoring the empty concrete picnic tables provided at the tiny deserted park. A narrow stream splashed peacefully over rocks nearby, the water sounds blending with the songs of the birds in the branches overhead. At six-thirty, the sun was still bright, the day still warm. Mallory was glad she'd thought of a picnic. Tugging at the baggy black cotton shorts she wore with a black-and-white striped pullover and black canvas sneakers, she sat Indian-style on one corner of the tablecloth, motioning for Elliott to do the same.

"The question is, is the traffic ready for me?" Elliott replied cautiously, adjusting his own beige poplin slacks to allow him to fold his long legs beneath him.

Mallory laughed as she opened the picnic hamper. "Don't be silly. You did very well today—with the exception of trying to climb a tree in a Ford," she added teasingly. "Tomorrow we'll get you a learner's permit so we can continue our lessons until you're ready for your license—which shouldn't take long at all, the way you've improved today. I can't believe it's taken you this long to get around to learning."

He shrugged, watching with interest as she pulled paper plates and plastic wrapped sandwiches from the basket. "You're a good teacher. The last time I tried to learn, it was in Chicago traffic in a car with a standard transmission and an instructor who got hysterical over every little thing. He'd have had a cerebral hemorrhage over that tree, rather than just chewing me out as you did."

Still smiling, Mallory continued to stack food on the cloth between them. "We'll have to take my dad's four-wheel-drive vehicle out sometime. Driving a standard's fun at times, particularly on four-wheel-drive trails. I think you might like it this time, particularly after you've had a bit more practice with an automatic."

"How many people did you plan to feed at this picnic?" Elliott asked in mild curiosity, staring doubtfully at the huge pile of food in front of him.

"I've got a big appetite," she returned with a flippant toss of her ponytail. "And it wouldn't hurt you to gain a few pounds."

He smiled without taking offense. "I could eat twice this much and not gain an ounce," he admitted. "I seem to burn up calories before I take them in."

"Lucky you. What kind of sandwich do you want first? We've got peanut butter and jelly or ham and cheese. Here, take one of each. This container has pickles, this one cherry tomatoes. We also have carrot sticks and—" she peeked beneath another plastic lid, then opened the bowl "—homemade cookies for dessert."

Elliott had been momentarily distracted by her legs, displayed to such nice advantage by her shorts and sneakers. Blinking, he accepted the loaded plate she held out to him with a murmured thanks, noting that she served herself equal amounts of the ultra-casual fare. He wondered if she, too, had a metabolism that allowed her to eat as much as she wanted and still stay so attractively slim. He bit into a sandwich, discovering that it was peanut butter and jelly. He hadn't eaten that mixture in years; he'd forgotten how much he'd once liked it. Washing it down with a long drink of the lukewarm canned soda she handed him, he almost choked when she asked airily, "By the way, how long have we known each other?"

Lowering the can, Elliott looked at her with a puzzled frown. "We met Monday. Why—"

"Oh, I don't mean in reality," she assured him quickly. "I meant what are we going to tell your family? They'll never believe this so-called love affair of ours has all come about in just three weeks."

"Yes, I guess you're right," he agreed. "How long *should* we have known each other?"

She shrugged. "Beats me." She took a bite of her own sandwich, chewed and swallowed as she considered his question. "A couple of months, I suppose. Would you have had time to date me during the past few weeks, or was Sybil always around?"

He shook his head in annoyance at her suggestion that Sybil never left his side. "Of course she wasn't always around. She's been dating George for months, going out with him several times a week. And she doesn't live with me. She has her own apartment. She doesn't always know what I do in the evenings."

"So you could have been seeing me without her knowledge."

"Yes."

"Why didn't you tell Sybil about me? She'll probably wonder why you never mentioned me to her."

Intrigued now by the variables of the charade they were planning, Elliott gave the question his full attention. "I was ashamed of you," he said at last, managing not to smile. "I was appalled to realize that a man of my intelligence had fallen for a cute, but scatterbrained secretary who—" He stopped, laughing, when Mallory threw a paper napkin at his head.

"Pig," she told him, though she was laughing with him, seemingly delighted by his teasing. "Try again."

Elliott was enjoying himself immensely. He rarely teased with anyone, other than Sybil, because most people treated him so deferentially, as if he would have no interest in anything but higher mathematics or computer science or world economics. Only with Mallory, and sometimes Sybil, could he laugh and even make fun of his own abilities. He hadn't realized how totally relaxing it could be just to sit cross-legged on a tablecloth by a stream, eating peanut butter sandwiches and trading good-natured insults.

"You were ashamed of me?" he suggested instead. "You were appalled to find yourself attracted to a nerd who—"

"Elliott, be serious. We need to discuss this. And besides," she added a bit gruffly, toying with a strip of plastic wrap, "you're not a nerd."

"You mean it's not totally inconceivable that you could be attracted to me—if I weren't your employer, of course?" he dared.

Still refusing to meet his eyes, she crumpled the plastic between her fingers. "No. Not inconceivable at all. So why didn't you tell Sybil about me?" she demanded hastily, refusing to pursue that particular line of conversation.

Oddly cheered by her words, he cooperated by offering a more serious suggestion. "I didn't want Sybil to interfere."

She lifted an eyebrow, which promptly disappeared behind her shaggy bangs. "Would she have?"

He groaned in answer. "If I'd told her I'd met someone I was very much attracted to, she would have insisted on meeting her, started to direct the romance, given me advice on what to say and do—and what *not* to say and do—made me go shopping for new clothes— she would have gone berserk," he concluded flatly. "I wanted a chance for our relationship to develop without outside distraction, so I simply didn't mention you to her."

"So why the decision to take me with you to Chicago?"

"I'm so crazy in love with you that I couldn't wait another day to start showing you off," he replied promptly, pleased that she blushed rosily at his answer.

"Maybe I asked to be introduced to your family," she proposed instead. "If you and I were getting serious, it would be normal for me to want to meet your sister and your grandparents."

"I suppose that would work," he agreed. "What other webs do we need to tangle now that we're practicing to deceive?"

She reached for a cookie. "That should just about do it, I think. We can say we met at a party."

"I never go to parties."

"Never?" she repeated in astonishment.

"Never. We met at the university library."

"But I don't attend the university. Why would I have been in the library?"

He conceded that she had a point.

"A grocery store?"

Elliott shook his head expressively.

"Of course," she said with a deep sigh. "You never go to grocery stores. I suppose shopping malls are out, too."

"Sybil buys all my clothes, and the housekeeper picks up the other stuff I need when she does the grocery shopping."

Mallory leaned back on her hands, and her knit top stretched snugly across her chest, almost distracting Elliott from their conversation. "Elliott, do you realize that if we hadn't met at that employment agency, we never would have met at all?"

He was just beginning to realize what a shame that would have been. "Don't give up, we'll think of something. Maybe a restaurant?"

She brightened. "I eat at restaurants."

He smiled. "So do I. Often alone. You were sitting at the table next to me—"

"And we bumped into each other when we got up to leave at the same time."

"I apologized."

"And we exchanged names, just to be polite."

"I walked you to your car to make sure you were okay."

She paused in their rapid exchange of possibilities. "Would you have done something like that?"

"I would have if you'd been wearing the dress you wore last night," he assured her, making no effort to hide his appreciative survey of her slender body.

Her throat worked as she swallowed. "And you worry about lacking flirting skills," she muttered.

"I told you," he reminded her gently, "I'm different with you than I am with other people. I never flirt with other women."

She eyed him reflectively. "I may just be creating a monster."

"You may just be right," he replied, pushing his plate aside and leaning toward her. This seemed as good a time as any to conduct the experiment he'd planned earlier.

Mallory's eyes grew wide as he loomed over her. "Um . . . Elliott?"

"Lesson two," he murmured, covering her mouth with his before she had a chance to make the objection he knew was coming.

The kiss the night before hadn't been a fluke. Whatever it was Mallory had done to him during that first kiss happened again as soon as their mouths met. He would have almost sworn he heard an orchestra playing, that fireworks were going off overhead in the gradually purpling sky. As often as he'd scorned such hackneyed descriptions when he'd read them in the past, he now realized where those romantic authors had gotten the inspiration for their flights of fancy. At some point in their lives, they must have shared kisses like this one.

Mallory made a little sound deep in her throat, whether pleasure or protest he wasn't sure, but her arms went tightly around his neck as they had the night before, her fingers sliding into his hair. He was hardly aware of shifting his weight, but suddenly they were lying full-length on the tablecloth, her body half-covered by his.

He had to breathe, but only for a moment. And then he was kissing her again, trying a new angle this time and finding it just as satisfying. His hand wandered from her waist upward, pausing just below the tempting swell of her left breast. He itched to move higher and cup that soft mound in his palm, but he was hesitant to do anything that would startle her into ending the interlude. He wanted to continue kissing her, to explore every centimeter of the sweet depths of her mouth. He moaned his approval when her lips parted to allow him access.

Mallory shifted recklessly beneath Elliott, her arms tightening around his neck as his tongue danced seductively with hers. She was all too aware of his hand lying so close to her involuntarily swelling breast. Even as she told herself she had to stop this insanity, she felt herself arching upward, straining to get closer to him.

For a man who proclaimed himself totally lacking in social skills, Elliott kissed like a dream.

At last the kiss ended. She was thoroughly chagrined to realize that it was he, not she, who brought it to a halt. Lifting his head, he looked down at her with glittering dark eyes, clearing his throat before speaking. "Well," he said, still a bit hoarse. "I guess that answers my question."

"What question?" she asked in little more than a whisper.

He shook his head, his smile crooked. "I'm not sure you'd understand."

She took a deep breath and brought her hands to his shoulders, shoving upward. When he sat up, she struggled upright, straightening her clothes. "This has got to stop," she told him firmly.

He didn't answer. Instead, he began to gather the remains of their dinner, stuffing them haphazardly into the picnic hamper.

"Elliott? Did you hear me?"

"Mmm. Hand me that bowl of carrot sticks, will you?"

She placed the bowl in his hand. "Elliott—"

"So what's the next step?"

"The what—?"

"You said you were going to teach me some social skills. What comes next?"

Trying to clear her kiss-clouded mind, she pushed her bangs off her forehead and wet her still-tender lips. "A party."

Elliott groaned.

Feeling somewhat more in control, Mallory stood. "That's right. I said I was going to introduce you to some people. My friends are having a party next Friday night. We're going."

"Mallory, I'm terrible at parties. I won't know what to say, how to act. I'll put a damper on everyone's fun."

"Don't be ridiculous. Just be yourself, Elliott. I've had a great time with you today. Everyone else will like you, too."

She noticed that he was beginning to look agitated. "I keep trying to tell you that I'm different with you. You've never seen me in a normal social situation. I'm hopeless."

Mallory scooped up the picnic hamper and headed for the car. "You're being absurd," she said, turning to Elliott. "You'll do fine. Now do you want to drive to your house or should I?"

He sighed and followed slowly, the tablecloth draped over his arm. "I'll drive. At least that's something I'm not totally inept at doing. But I still think this party's a terrible idea."

"Elliott, I'm trusting you to drive my car, remember? Now trust me a little. The party's going to be great."

"Just don't say I didn't warn you," Elliott muttered, turning the key in the ignition and shoving the gearshift into reverse.

4

"IT'S GOING TO BE a disaster. You'll be sorry, I promise you."

Mallory sighed and threw up her hands in exasperation. "Would you stop saying that?" she demanded of her pessimistic employer, who perched on the side of her desk looking gloomy. "You've been predicting disaster all week, and I keep telling you that you're wrong. The party tonight is going to be fun. For both of us."

Elliott folded his arms across his chest and scowled. "Just don't say I didn't warn you."

"You've warned me," she agreed. "About seventy-jillion times. So enough, already."

He shrugged in an I've-done-all-I-can-do gesture and let the subject drop. "What are your plans for lunch today?" he asked instead.

"Nothing special. Why?"

"Consider yourself booked for lunch." He stood, ran his hand through his hair and smiled down at her. "I've got some calls to make. I'll be in the pit if you need me."

Mallory chuckled at the name she'd given his office and which Elliott had promptly adopted. Watching him leave, she thought rather smugly that he'd come a long way in the past week. He'd made a special effort to be easier to work for, though working for Elliott would never be quite like working for a normal businessman, she thought in cheerful resignation. He'd continued the teasing they'd begun on the driving lesson last Saturday, frequently making her laugh at his dry wit.

There had been three afternoon repeats of that lesson, and she'd been amazed at how quickly he'd picked up the skill once he'd been convinced that it was something he needed to learn and had the potential to do well.

How she wanted to yell at his family for treating him like a brilliant incompetent for most of his life! Brilliant he was, but he was also a human being with human feelings, something his family seemed to have overlooked quite often.

Since the driving lessons had usually extended into shared dinners, Mallory had learned quite a bit about Elliott during the past five days. Enough to know that he'd often felt isolated, different, lonely. She'd often experienced the same feelings and deeply sympathized—something she had to keep in perspective, she reminded herself. There had been no repeats of the two mind-blowing kisses they'd shared, but it hadn't been for lack of trying on Elliott's part. Mallory had become quite skilled at reading amorous intent in his gorgeous dark eyes and distracting him with an unexpectedly outrageous stunt or comment. She freely admitted she was a coward. It would take very few of Elliott's kisses to smash into dust whatever shaky willpower she maintained around him.

Leaning her elbows on her desktop, she propped her chin on her fists and stared into space, reminding herself of all the reasons she could *not* become romantically involved with Elliott Fraser. She'd learned her lesson with Larry, the handsome, charming, wealthy employer who'd entertained himself for a time with his amusing secretary. Mallory had fallen in love with the same wholehearted enthusiasm with which she did everything else, only to be shocked by a newspaper announcement of Larry's engagement to a rich, prominent Dallas socialite. When she'd confronted Larry with the announcement, he'd coolly informed her that he'd never had any intention of marrying a mere office worker, that a man like him married within his own social circles. He'd then implied that his relationship with Mallory needn't change simply because he would be marrying another woman.

Infuriated at his offer to make her his mistress, Mallory had left him with a roundhouse punch that had almost dislocated his jaw. It had almost broken her hand, as well, but she'd never regretted it.

What was it about her that made her susceptible to men so totally different from herself? She was doing it again with Elliott. Not only was he extremely wealthy, but he was also an acclaimed intellectual. His world was totally different from her own. He was attracted to her, of course. She'd have to be blind and stupid not to notice. But she firmly believed that he, like Larry, would eventually choose a woman more like himself for a permanent mate. Another genius, probably, like that woman in his think tank. Mallory was a novelty, a tool he was using for the task of ensuring his sister's happiness. Once he no longer needed her, he'd move on to someone more his mental and social equal.

"Mallory? Is something wrong?"

Startled, she focused on the concerned face in front of her. When had Elliott come back into her office? she wondered, straightening abruptly and trying to look efficient. "Of course not, Elliott. I was just preparing myself to begin the McClellan report. What can I do for you?"

He continued to frown down at her. "Preparing yourself to type a report? That's what made you look so sad? You shouldn't do it if you dread it so badly, Mallory. I can have it done at the university."

Again, he was taking her words much too literally. Feeling unreasonably guilty, Mallory shook her head and spoke rather gruffly. "Don't be silly. Doing your typing is my job, remember? And I don't dislike it. You simply caught me daydreaming for a few minutes, that's all. Was there something you needed, Elliott?"

He nodded slowly. "A pencil. Mine have all disappeared again."

She pulled out her desk drawer and handed him two newly sharpened number-two pencils. "There you go. I'll dig more out of the rubble in the pit later this afternoon. Anything else?"

"No. That's all. You're sure you're okay?"

"Positive," she replied firmly. "Now go away, Elliott. I have typing to do before lunch."

She relaxed in relief when he did as she ordered. Turning to the computer keyboard, she began the report, telling herself that she was going to have to stop mooning over her sexy, unattainable boss before she made a complete fool of herself. Again.

PROMPTLY AT TWELVE, Elliott appeared in Mallory's office to carry her off to lunch. Something about the gleam in his eyes made her wonder just what it was he was up to. "Where are we going?" she asked as she slid into the passenger seat of her car. Elliott wanted to drive.

"You'll see," he promised, confidently guiding the Ford onto the highway.

Mallory's puzzled frown vanished when he pulled into a huge Chevrolet dealership. "You're buying a car!"

"Right the first time," he approved, slanting her a grin. "I want you to help me pick one out. I've discovered I'm tired of waiting for cabs."

"Oh, this is going to be fun," Mallory said happily, her eyes already scanning the huge array of vehicles displayed for purchase. It didn't seem at all unusual to her to buy a car during lunch hour—that was the way she'd bought her Ford, after all. "Why Chevy?" she asked casually as she and Elliott climbed out of her car.

He shrugged. "I want to buy American. A Ford or Chrysler would be just as suitable, I suppose. If we don't find anything here, we'll try one of the others."

She nodded, already walking toward a grouping of luxurious, businessman-type vehicles that seemed appropriate for Elliott. She watched as a hungry-looking young salesman approached, his eyes sparkling with the fever of a potential sale. "How're you folks doing?" he inquired in a broad East Texas drawl, one hand in the pocket of his inexpensive polyester slacks as he extended the other to Elliott. "Looking for a car?"

Resisting the impulse to tell the guy that no, they were hoping to find a horse and buggy, Mallory smiled and said nothing as Elliott murmured something fitting. She wandered over to a particularly attractive metallic blue vehicle and opened the driver's door to examine the plush interior. Yes, she thought, it looked like a car Elliott would like.

"Ah, the missus has good taste," the salesman, who'd introduced himself as Jimmy, approved heartily, moving immediately to Mallory's side. "It's a beauty, isn't it? Got all the options. Tilt wheel, adjustable seats—just touch that button right there—cruise control, AM-FM with tape deck, plush seats, carpet . . ."

He went on for almost fifteen minutes, non-stop. Listening with only half her attention, Mallory walked slowly around the car, then climbed into it, testing the comfort of the seats. Lots of room for Elliott's long legs, she thought, stretching her own as far as they'd go.

"This one's nice, Elliott. Elliott?" She poked her head out the door and then climbed out to look for him. "Elliott?"

She spotted him halfway across the lot, his backside sticking out of the opened hood of a sleek gold sports car. Jimmy was beside him, speaking rapidly and using lots of hand motions. Mallory's eyes widened. A Corvette? For a man whose idea of flashy clothing was poplin slacks and a polo shirt?

Elliott's expression was decidedly sheepish when Mallory joined him beside the car. "I—uh—noticed it from over there," he explained diffidently. "Pretty color, isn't it?"

"It's gorgeous," she replied immediately. "I just didn't expect you to be interested in a sports car."

He looked toward the row of larger, more conservative cars. "You're right, of course. One of those would be much more practical."

Mallory couldn't help laughing at the wistful expression on his face. He looked like a little boy in a toy store who felt obligated to select an educational toy when what he really wanted was a skateboard. "Let's look at this one," she said, heading for the driver's door.

Ignoring Jimmy, who'd gone into a sales frenzy at the thought of such a large commission, she slid behind the wheel, snuggling blissfully into the soft black leather bucket seat. She noted the automatic transmission with satisfaction, not quite sure Elliott was ready for five-in-the-floor. "Oh, wow," she murmured, eyeing the aviation-style dash with its many gauges and indicators. "This is incredible."

"You like it?" Elliott asked with not-very-well concealed eagerness, leaning into the door beside her.

"It's flashy, overpriced, juvenile and totally impractical," she replied, watching from the corner of her eye as his mouth drooped in disappointment. "And," she added, breaking into a smile, "I think you should buy it."

His eyes lit up. "Really?"

"Of course. It's perfect. Exactly what you need in your life. Too bad we're not driving to Chicago so you could spring it on your family."

Elliott grinned. "They'd choke."

"Yes," she agreed happily. "They probably would."

She was in for another mild shock when Elliott casually wrote a check for the full price of the vehicle. She'd be making payments on her economy Ford for eighteen more months—and she'd bought it used, she thought with a sigh that she hoped wasn't too envious. After making a quick call to the bank, the dealership manager did everything but kiss Elliott's hand, promising the car would be ready for delivery that very afternoon.

"That's a real understanding wife you got there," Jimmy confided in Elliott as they walked back to Mallory's Ford. "*My* ball and chain would've had a fit if I'd picked something sporty instead of practical. You're a lucky guy."

Rather than correcting the salesman's misapprehension, Elliott only nodded, grinning at Mallory's pink cheeks. "Yes, I am, aren't I?"

Mallory concentrated on her watch as Elliott guided her car away from the dealership, promising to find a quick place to eat before returning to the office. They'd stopped at the dealership just under an hour before, which meant he'd spent about five hundred dollars for every minute they'd been there, she rapidly calculated. Gulping, she commented hastily, "Of course you know that you'll have to get a driver's license now, don't you? Your permit requires that you have a licensed driver in the car with you. I'll come with you this afternoon to pick up your car."

"Not necessary," Elliott assured her, with what could only be called a smug smile.

Mallory frowned at him. "Elliott, you can't drive without a license. You'll get a ticket."

Shifting his weight, he pulled his wallet from his back pocket and tossed it in her lap. "Open it."

"Elliott! You got your license! But when?"

"This morning," he answered with a broad grin.

"I thought you were at the university this morning."

"I know. I wanted to surprise you."

"You did." She leaned over impulsively to kiss his cheek. "Congratulations. I've never known anyone else who learned to drive *and* got a license all in less than a week."

Lips tingling from the contact with his skin, she sat back in her seat, managing not to laugh when he blushed at her compliment.

Elliott drove for a few minutes in silence, then slanted her a quick glance. "You really like the car I picked out?"

"Very much," she assured him.

"You can drive it to the party tonight after I pick you up," he promised.

She grinned in anticipation. "Really? You'll let me drive it?"

He chuckled. "I'd be a jerk not to after you've so unselfishly taught me to drive and let me practice in your car, wouldn't I?"

She only smiled, settling back into her seat. Not a jerk, she thought happily, looking at the attractive man beside her and allowing herself one quick moment of feminine appreciation. Definitely not a jerk.

ELLIOTT TURNED OFF the ignition and sat behind the wheel of his Corvette, staring gloomily at Mallory's apartment. He really hated parties, he thought, sighing his resignation as he climbed out of the low-slung car, carefully closing the door behind him. Wasting just a moment admiring his new toy, he finally patted the hood and headed grimly to pick up his date for the dreaded event.

"Right on time," Mallory approved as she opened her door, smiling up at him.

She looked great, he decided, eyeing her trendy, emerald-green cotton jumpsuit with its wide belt and rakish collar, the front buttons opened far enough to show just a shadowy hint of cleavage. She'd substituted a complicated-looking braid for her usual ponytail, making him realize that he'd never seen her hair loose—and stirring a strong desire in him to do just that. He'd bet it would look great fanned across a pillow.

Gulping at his immediate and unexpectedly physical reaction to the errant thought, he pulled his eyes firmly back to her face, only to note the hint of disapproval in her eyes as she studied his appearance. "What's wrong?" he asked, looking down at his dark suit, silk shirt and tie. "I thought I was very careful to match colors. My socks are the same color as my suit, so—"

"It's not that," she cut in. "And you look very nice. It's just that you're a bit overdressed for the occasion. I told you the party is informal."

He scowled. "I thought you meant that formal evening clothes wouldn't be necessary. I'll go change, if you think I should. Or better yet, we can forget the whole evening."

She waggled her finger at him in good-natured reproof. "Nice try, but forget it. You can just leave the tie and coat in the car and you'll be fine."

"I won't be fine," he muttered, following her to his car. "I'll be miserable. I hate parties. I don't know what to say, how to act. How am I supposed to talk to strangers who have nothing at all in common with me?"

"Small talk," she advised, patting his arm. "It's called meeting people, making friends. It's easy."

"For you, maybe," he returned doubtfully.

"You can do it, Elliott."

Reaching his car, he turned and abruptly pulled her into his arms. There in the parking lot, he held her full-length against him and kissed her until an odd humming noise in his ears warned him that he'd better pull back. Reluctantly, he did, though he kept his hands loosely at her waist.

Panting for breath, her eyes enormous, Mallory stared up at him. "What—what was that for?" she asked, her voice rather squeaky.

"False courage."

She took a deep breath, drawing his eyes again to the low neckline of her jumpsuit, and shook her head reprovingly at him. "That's supposed to come from alcohol, not kisses."

"But kisses taste so much better," he replied logically, his mouth hovering just above hers. And then he kissed her again before he could blurt out that her kisses were much more intoxicating than any mere alcoholic drink.

"WHERE IN THE WORLD did you find him, Mallory?"

Mallory smiled somewhat ruefully at the shapely brunette standing beside her in the gold-and-white papered powder room. "He's my boss," she answered, not needing clarification of the *him* in Cindy's question.

"Ah." Cindy nodded, seeming to suddenly understand. "So are you trying to soften him up for a raise? A promotion? Is *that* why you're going out with him?" Blatantly materialistic, unapologetically lax in ethical principles, Cindy could perfectly understand such reasons for Mallory to be dating her employer.

Knowing Cindy too well to be offended, but feeling compelled to defend Elliott, Mallory shook her head. "He's really very nice, Cindy. I'm with Elliott tonight because I enjoy being with him." She had no intention of trying to explain the agreement she'd made with Elliott about teaching him to be more adaptable to the normal world. For one thing, Cindy would be sure to point out that Mallory wasn't doing such a great job so far.

She wasn't surprised that Cindy's eyes widened in disbelief when Mallory said she enjoyed Elliott's company. During the past two hours, Elliott had certainly made no effort to demonstrate the warm, relaxed side of himself that Mallory had come to know and appreciate. From the moment he'd entered the large, sprawling ranch-style house in which the party was being held, Elliott had acted like a stiff, awkward, somewhat disapproving professor being forced to chaperone a fraternity bash. Mallory had introduced him to many people, nice people despite their diversities, but Elliott had spoken very little, and seemed unwilling—or unable—to blend in. And, though she'd reminded him of his promise to practice his dancing, he'd yet to even make the attempt, taking one look at the crowded impromptu dance floor and flatly refusing to step onto it.

"You said he's a professor of some sort?" Cindy asked, touching her ruby-nailed little finger to the corner of her glossed-to-match mouth as she leaned closer to the lighted mirror over the marble vanity.

"Yes. And an inventor. He's very intelligent—very highly respected in the academic world," Mallory enthused.

"Mmm. Not bad looking, either. But much too dull for my taste." Cindy smoothed her sequin-studded dress over her voluptuous figure and shot Mallory a wicked, laughing glance. "A girl would probably have to take a magazine to bed to have something to entertain herself with while he—"

"Cindy!" Mallory protested, beginning to get annoyed with the bluntly outspoken woman. "That's not at all nice."

"Well, honestly, Mallory, can you imagine going to bed with that stiff-necked, scowling professor?" Cindy shuddered delicately as she asked the question. "He probably learned lovemaking out of a textbook on the human reproductive system."

Now Mallory was angry, oddly protective of the man Cindy was maligning. "As a matter of fact, I *can* imagine making love with Elliott," she retorted haughtily. She'd spent a great deal of time lately imagining just that, though she didn't bother to let Cindy know. "And you might just be surprised by him. I know his kisses have the power to melt *my* kneecaps!"

Tossing her head, she turned on that revelation and swept from the room, leaving Cindy looking startled and decidedly intrigued.

HANDS SHOVED IN HIS POCKETS, Elliott slouched against a wall in the corner he'd claimed for himself in the crowded room and glumly watched Mallory make her way toward him. It was taking a while, as she was stopped by nearly everyone she passed for quick, laughing conversations. His eyes narrowed as one darkly handsome male caught her for a quick hug. Mallory didn't seem to mind the liberty—just the opposite, in fact. She laughed and returned the hug just as heartily, her smile brilliant as she chattered vivaciously.

Elliott hated the guy.

The party was a disaster. Hadn't he said it would be? She just wouldn't believe him when he'd told her that he was completely inept in situations like this one. He'd be perfectly at home, of course, at a gathering of scientists or economists—even if they were complete strangers to him. But he had no idea how he should behave at this noisy, rowdy bash. Unlike Mallory or her friends, who had come into the room knowing what to expect, how to act, what to say to make the others laugh in warm approval. As far as Elliott could tell, there wasn't a serious conversation going on anywhere in the room—unless one counted the extremely serious looking discussion going on between one couple in a far corner, and Elliott would bet his most sophisticated scientific calculator that *their* discussion belonged in the nearest bedroom.

His eyes returned to Mallory. She was so vibrant, so very much alive. Even as he ached to catch her into his arms for another hard, potent kiss, he told himself that he had nothing to offer her, no reason to expect her to return his rapidly developing feelings for her. She was a colorful, free-spirited hummingbird, zipping from flower to flower in a zestful celebration of life; he was a sober brown owl, sitting on a lonely branch observing her erratic flight. How long would he be able to hold her—if at all—before she dashed off in search of more excitement, more gaiety, leaving his life emptier and more colorless than ever before?

He wanted her. He'd never wanted another woman with the intensity of his desire for Mallory. He'd never lain awake at night, his body hard and throbbing, covered in sweat as he fought mental pictures straight out of an x-rated movie. For that matter, he'd never even *seen* an x-rated movie, but he was quite sure some of his fantasies during the past few nights could compare quite adequately. He wanted her. And yet . . .

Would she find him a good lover? The women he'd been with in the past had seemed satisfied enough afterward, but they'd been different—more like himself. Mallory would be as adventurous, as uninhibited and zestful in bed as she was in daily life. Could he please her? Would she find him lacking in comparison to past lovers? Would she be left dissatisfied, even bored? Again, he found himself in a sweat, but this a cold one, born of uncertain misgiving. Did he have the courage to take the risk, to open himself to rejection?

Mallory reached him before he could find an answer to his own anguished question. Rather than looking annoyed with him, as well she should, she smiled sympathetically and lifted a soft hand to his cheek. "Poor Elliott. Are you really as miserable as you look?"

Rigid with the effort not to reach out and drag her into his arms, he managed a shrug that he hoped seemed cool and detached. "I tried to tell you this wasn't my kind of affair."

"Yes, I know you did. I'm sorry I pushed you into it. Are you ready to go?"

He was more than ready to go. He swallowed guiltily. "I hate to ruin your evening."

She shook her head, dropping her hand to slip it under his arm. "Don't be silly. Let's blow this joint."

He smiled at her teasing, the first smile he'd managed since they'd arrived. Turning with her toward the door, he swallowed a groan when they were detained by a flashily attractive brunette Mallory had introduced him to earlier. He remembered that her name was Cindy, but he wondered why she was suddenly eyeing him with new speculation. She'd made no effort to hide her total lack of interest when they'd met earlier.

She didn't leave him wondering for long. After asking if they were already leaving and being answered in the affirmative, she looked at Elliott with a beckoning, almost feline smile. "I won't ask what your hurry is. If your kisses are as good as Mallory said, I don't blame her for rushing you off to herself."

"Cindy!" Mallory blurted, sounding a bit choked as she scolded the gaily amused woman.

Elliott felt his cheeks darkening with an unaccustomed flush. He couldn't help slanting Mallory a questioning look. So she thought he kissed well, did she? One corner of his mouth twitched as she met his eyes with a rueful wince.

Cindy reached out one long-nailed hand to stroke Elliott's arm. "Maybe you'll give me a demonstration sometime?" she asked audaciously.

Startled by her bold teasing, Elliott looked down at her, wondering what the hell he was supposed to say. Several people standing around them had overheard her remarks and were muffling laughter as they waited for a response from the unsociable professor. From out of nowhere, a mischievous impulse gripped him, making him smile slightly, quirk an eyebrow and run his eyes slowly up and down the well-built brunette. "Maybe I'll do that sometime," he murmured in what he hoped was a Clark Gable voice. "If you're lucky."

Cindy's dramatically made up eyes widened, then narrowed in genuine intrigue. The eavesdroppers around them laughed approvingly and began to tease Cindy. Mallory muttered something unintelligible and pulled on Elliott's arm, almost dragging him out of the room beside her.

Strangely pleased with himself, Elliott smiled as he escorted his still-flushed and slightly disgruntled date to his car. Maybe he could learn to adapt, after all. With just a little more practice....

His smile faded as he climbed into his car beside Mallory, who was unusually quiet and withdrawn.

And then again, he thought, maybe not.

5

MALLORY FOUND HERSELF frowning and fidgeting as she dressed for work Monday morning. She hadn't heard from Elliott since Friday evening, not since he'd left her at her door after the party without even a good-night kiss. Not that she'd given him much chance to do anything else, she admitted candidly. Embarrassed and upset by Cindy's tactless teasing, Mallory had been strangely shy around Elliott on the way home. He, too, had withdrawn into his own thoughts, his expression unreadable.

He'd had a lousy time at the party. Had he blamed Mallory? Was he regretting the bargain they'd made, wishing he'd never mentioned his problems with his family? Or had he been intrigued by Cindy's blatant pass, wondering how soon he could take her up on her not-so-subtle offer?

"Give her a demonstration, indeed," she muttered, savagely brushing her freshly washed hair. And then she scowled again as she remembered Elliott's smug reply. *"If you're lucky.* He stands there like a lump all evening, then turns into a smooth-talking flirt just as we're ready to leave. Now Cindy will probably knock herself out to arrange another encounter with Elliott. Probably thinks there's enough potential there that she'd be just the one to bring him out of his shell."

Realizing she was grumbling into her mirror, she sighed in self-disgust and dropped the hairbrush, catching her hair in both hands and twisting it into her usual modified ponytail.

She'd missed him during the past two days. She'd found herself standing by the telephone Sunday evening wishing he'd call, wondering if she should dial his number with some casual excuse just to talk to him. And she'd been stunned to realize how much she'd enjoyed being with him during the past weeks, how strongly she was beginning to feel for him. It wouldn't do, she'd told herself then, and she reaffirmed the decision now. It simply wouldn't do at all.

It was time to pull back, to keep a friendly distance from Elliott before she became too deeply involved with him. He'd made it quite clear Friday evening that they had little in common, that he wasn't particularly interested in fitting into her world, and she knew she'd never fit into his. She'd told herself all along, but the party had served as a vivid illustration of that very point. So, she would be polite, cool, efficient, as helpful to him as possible, but she would remain aloof, protect herself from his attractive charms. No more kisses, no more late-night fantasizing.

And maybe, when they returned from Chicago, she'd better start job hunting again. Something told her that she hadn't a chance in Hades of resisting Elliott when she couldn't even be in the same room with him without melting into her penny loafers.

"GOOD MORNING, MALLORY."

Mallory inclined her head in response to Elliott's polite greeting as he entered her office later that day, after spending most of the morning at the university. He'd already been gone when she'd arrived for work, much to her relief. "Good morning, Elliott."

"Any messages?"

She reached for a neat stack of pink papers. "Yes, several. Would you like me to go through them with you?"

He shook his head, avoiding her eyes. "No, I'll take care of them. Thank you. If you—if you need anything, I'll be in my office."

Not 'the pit' today, she noted, her throat tightening at his formality. "All right." The telephone on her desk buzzed and she reached for it. By the time she'd concluded the call with the hopeful stockbroker—a call she didn't even have to ask if Elliott wanted to take—Elliott had disappeared into the depths of his office.

His door was still closed when she returned from lunch. She paused in front of it, wistfully thinking of him inside, then resolutely marched to her own desk and settled back down to work. An hour later he approached her desk, still with that total lack of expression that actually made her ache to look at him. "Do you need something, Elliott?"

"The Hollister file," he answered quietly. "Have you seen it, by any chance?"

"Yes. I'll get it for you." She found the file quickly, handing it to him with her eyes fixed somewhere around his Adam's apple, careful to avoid a meeting of fingers as the file changed hands.

"Thank you."

"You're welcome."

"I'll—uh—I'll be in my office."

"Fine."

Her throat was tight when she returned to her chair, her eyes strangely hot.

Another hour passed before they spoke again. And then it was only through the intercom. "Elliott," Mallory announced diffidently, pressing the button on her telephone. "Dr. Carlson is on line one. Do you want to take the call?"

"Yes, of course. Um—thank you."

"You're welcome." The words seemed to strain her throat, which had grown even tighter. She found herself blinking back tears as she turned to her keyboard.

By the end of the next hour she knew something had to be done. She couldn't go on like this. Shoving herself out of her chair, she marched resolutely to the doorway, intending to storm Elliott's office for a confrontation. She was going to find out once and for all if he was sorry he'd ever met her.

They almost bumped into each other in the hallway as Elliott came stamping out of his office at almost the exact moment Mallory left hers.

"Elliott, I—"

"Mallory, I—"

They stopped, staring at each other. "You go ahead," Elliott urged.

Her courage deserted her abruptly. "No, you first," she insisted weakly.

He stubbornly shook his head. "I can wait. What was it you wanted?"

They were being so carefully polite she wanted to spit. Near tears only minutes before, she now found herself fighting the urge to laugh. She swallowed hard, but the giggles escaped through the fingers she clamped over her mouth.

Elliott frowned. "You're laughing," he accused, as if she weren't aware of the fact.

His tone did her in. "I'm sorry," she gasped, holding her side. "It's just—" Her voice broke as she was overcome by another spasm of giggling.

Elliott made an oddly choked sound and then he, too, was laughing, leaning against the wall. "I know why you're laughing," he admitted when he'd recovered sufficiently to speak. "We've both been acting like a couple of idiots today, haven't we?"

She nodded, wiping futilely at her streaming eyes. "We were so polite it was nauseating. I almost called you 'sir' once."

He chuckled again. "I'm not sure I could have handled that. I was beginning to believe you weren't really Mallory Littlefield at all, but an android sent here to scramble my brains. Thank God you're back to normal."

"And you," she agreed gravely, though her mouth still tilted crookedly upward. "If you'd said 'thank you' one more time, I would have sworn you were on something. We've never been that formal with each other before."

"No."

"Elliott, I—"

"Mallory, I—"

They laughed again. And then Elliott straightened, his jaw set in determination. "Be quiet a minute, will you? I've got something to say."

She smiled happily and complied.

Elliott reached out to take her shoulders in his hands, his dark eyes locked with hers. "I'm sorry about Friday evening. I ruined the party for you, and it was entirely my own fault. I went in with an attitude of defeat, and I didn't even try to make it work. You were trying to help me, and I made no effort whatever to help myself."

She raised her hands to his chest, anxiously looking up at him. "No, Elliott, I'm the one who's sorry. I pushed you into a situation that made you uncomfortable. You told me all along that you didn't want to go, but I completely ignored you. It was unforgivably presumptuous of me."

"Look, let's not stand here arguing about whose fault it was," Elliott said impatiently. "Yell at me or something, will you, before we start being polite and nauseating again?"

She smiled, impulsively slipping her arms around his waist to hug him. "I'll yell at you later. Right now I'm just glad we're friends again."

"Sure," Elliott agreed, his voice rather strained. "Friends." His arms tightened for just a moment around her before he stepped back, putting several feet between them. "Now, about those dancing lessons—"

"I promise not to nag you about dancing again," she replied lightly, trying to hide the sudden trembling in her hands by clenching them behind her. Her entire body felt warm from that all-too-brief contact with his.

"I want to learn," he argued firmly. "There will be dancing at my grandparents' anniversary party, and I don't intend to stand on the sidelines like a wallflower the way I did Friday night. What do you say to private lessons? Here. We can start tonight if you have no other plans."

She studied him warily. "You really want to learn to dance?"

"Yes. I do," he answered without hesitation. "Will you teach me?"

"Of course I will." She couldn't have denied his request, despite her misgivings at being alone in his home that evening, being held in his arms as they danced. Her hands trembled harder at the provocative picture.

Friends, she reminded herself doggedly. Just friends. *Sure.*

ELLIOTT KNEW the basic steps to the most popular ballroom dances—a skill that had been drilled into him as a youth, he admitted glumly. But, as Mallory informed him bluntly, he moved as if he had a poker stuck up his backside. "Loosen up," she urged him. "Feel the music. Glide with it."

He glided right onto her foot.

"Ouch!"

Sighing gustily, Elliott dropped his arms from around her and stepped back, shaking his head in disgust. "I'm sorry. Sybil always said I had all the grace of a pregnant elephant."

Mallory lifted her chin in renewed determination, surreptitiously rubbing her bruised right instep against the back of her left leg. "Forget what Sybil says. You're just a bit rusty from lack of practice, that's all. We've only been at this for twenty minutes or so. You're doing fine."

Darn that family of his. Mallory had a sudden urge to take each one of his loving relatives in hand for a fierce shaking. Had he been nothing more than a brain to them? Couldn't any of them see that he was vulnerable and uncertain in areas other than the intellectual? Another equally strong impulse made her want to throw her arms around him and simply hold him, but she managed to resist that one. Instead, she thought of the movie *Dirty Dancing*, trying to remember the tricks Johnny Castle has used to teach Baby to dance. She smiled as she considered the odds of turning Elliott into a performance-level dancer in as short a time as had passed in the Hollywood fantasy. She'd better settle for teaching him to get by at his grandparents' anniversary party.

"Let's try again," she suggested, setting the needle back down on the record she'd provided and turning to him with an encouraging smile.

Something about the way she looked at him made Elliott's chest tighten. Such optimism sparkled in her expressive green eyes, such confidence in his ability to do whatever he set his mind to doing. Was she really that sure of him? What was it she saw in him that no one else had?

He reached out to take her into his arms, but rather than assuming a dancing position, he pulled her against him for a quick, hard hug, his eyes closing as he pressed his face to her hair. There was nothing sexual in his gesture, though he was fully aware of every inch of her compact body pressed to his. He only wanted to hold her for a moment.

Mallory was a bit flushed when he released her, looking up at him with an uncertain smile. "What was that for?"

"Consider it a thank you for not giving up on me," he answered as casually as possible, sliding one hand to her waist as he took her right hand in his and prepared to dance.

Her smile became brilliant. She took him completely by surprise when she went up on her tiptoes to press a quick kiss on his lips. "Consider that 'you're welcome,'" she murmured. Before he could respond, she became all business, giving him dancing instructions in a brisk, matter-of-fact tone that encouraged no further intimacies.

SOMETIME AROUND THREE the next morning, Mallory stood at her bedroom window, staring out at the clear black sky decorated with a gleaming half moon and twinkling stars. The tangled bedcovers behind her testified to the hours she'd spent tossing and turning, trying to sleep, but tormented by memories of being held in Elliott's arms, their lips touching so briefly, so unsatisfactorily. He hadn't kissed her when she'd left him, nor had she given him any indication that she was willing for him to do so.

Just friends, she reminded herself.

So why was she throbbing all over with the need to be close to him again, closer than mere dancing permitted?

She groaned and pressed her hot cheek to the cool glass of the window, her eyes closing as she futilely fought the intimate images flashing through her mind.

At approximately the same time, Elliott stood under a cold shower, bracing himself against the tile wall with one stiffened arm as he turned his face into the spray. The cool water was doing little to ease the heat of his body. All he had to do was think of Mallory for the blood to surge hotly through him again, arousing him to a painful throbbing state. And, despite his best efforts, he couldn't stop thinking of Mallory. Of her smile, her laughter, her contagious enthusiasm. Her soft, full lips, her sleek, feminine curves. The feel of her in his arms. The way she looked at him with what he could almost believe was the same simmering desire he felt each time he looked at her.

He groaned loudly, dropping his head until the water streamed down his face and chest, splashing onto his back at the same time. He couldn't start deluding himself about her feelings for him, he reminded himself sternly. She'd made it quite clear that she wanted to be his friend, and nothing more. And, knowing she was probably right about her reasons, he'd agreed.

And still he wanted her until he thought he'd explode from it. Cursing savagely beneath his breath, he twisted the shower knobs to turn off the water and snatched at a towel. So much for the legendary advantages of a cold shower. It would take more than icy water to dampen the heat Mallory generated in him.

ELLIOTT PATIENTLY SIGNED the stack of neatly typed letters, half-sitting on Mallory's desk as he did so. One by one he handed them to her after scrawling his name at the bottom, until the last of the letters was signed. Capping the pen, he looked up at her. "What else?"

She referred to her calendar. "Don't forget that you have that meeting with Dr. Hawkes in the morning at nine. Oh, and you have a faculty reception Thursday evening at eight."

Elliott groaned. "Let's forget about that one."

She looked up with a quick frown. "You promised Dr. Carlson you'd be there, Elliott."

"He caught me at a weak moment."

"Still, you really should go." She smiled. "How bad can it be, compared to last Friday night? At least at *this* gathering you'll know everyone and have the university in common with them."

He rubbed his chin meditatively, deciding to make the best of it. "I'll go on one condition."

"What's that?"

"You go with me. As my date."

Her eyes widened comically. "You want *me* to go with you to a faculty reception? Oh, Elliott, I can't—"

"I went to your party with you," he reminded her without remorse at using her own guilt against her.

She narrowed her eyes at him. "Are you trying to blackmail me into going?"

"Whatever it takes," he replied cheerfully. "Is that a yes?"

Though her lower lip protruded in a pout that almost shattered his already fragile willpower, she nodded. "I guess so. But I won't know how to act with a bunch of professors. I'll be totally out of place."

"How bad can it be, compared to last Friday night?" he quoted her, managing with some effort not to grab her and taste her innocently seductive pout.

"All right. You win. I'll go with you."

He smiled at the lack of enthusiasm in her words. "Consider it a dress rehearsal," he suggested. "We'll be leaving for Chicago the next day, when we're supposed to begin our masquerade of the happy couple. We can practice a bit Thursday evening."

She was already fighting a smile, accepting the situation with her usual good grace. "It'll be a disaster," she predicted in a blatant imitation of him.

He only laughed and shoved himself to his feet. "How about having dinner with me tonight before our next dancing lesson? The least I can do to repay you is to buy you a meal at your favorite restaurant."

"You're on," she agreed without hesitation. "I hope you like Italian."

"Sure. Where do you want to go?"

"The Spaghetti Warehouse."

He'd heard of the popular west-end restaurant, but he'd never eaten there. He wasn't at all surprised that Mallory's favorite restaurant was a trendy, casual place frequented by tourists and an eclectic mixture of Dallas natives. "All right. I'll pick you up at seven. That'll give you time to freshen up after work."

"Fine."

Elliott was smiling as he left her office. He actually found himself having to fight the urge to whistle. Odd. He wasn't a whistler. As a matter of fact, he couldn't whistle a tune if his life depended on it. He shook his head in amazement at the changes Mallory had made in him in such a short time.

THE SPAGHETTI WAREHOUSE wasn't Elliott's usual type of restaurant, but he adapted easily enough to the noisy, exuberant atmosphere. He hardly raised an eyebrow at the mismatched furnishings, the booths made of white iron bedsteads, or the old-style arcade they passed as they followed the hostess toward the back of the huge place. Without comment, he ducked his head as they were led into the old railway car in the center of the table-crowded floor in the back of the restaurant. The car had been furnished with ten tables, each set to hold four diners. Removing two place settings from one of the tables, the hostess motioned for them to be seated and handed them their menus.

Mallory noted that Elliott wasn't quite certain what to make of the restaurant's ambience, but he had no complaints at all about the food—crisp salads, scrumptious pasta dishes, warm San Francisco-style sourdough bread. And though they had to raise their voices slightly above the cheerful din surrounding them, they talked easily through dinner, laughing frequently.

It pleased Mallory that Elliott seemed genuinely interested in her opinions, even on such serious topics as politics and future technologies, about which she was admittedly naive. She could have listened to him talk on any subject for hours; he was interesting and informative without once sounding condescending or lecturing. She had a wonderful time, despite the aching sensation somewhere in the region of her heart at the thought that she wouldn't always have Elliott around. She'd gotten much too spoiled by his company, she decided.

The carefully maintained camaraderie continued through the dancing lesson at Mallory's apartment after dinner. There wasn't as much room for dancing in her living room as there had been at his place the evening before, but she was pleased with the progress he was making. Again she was impressed with his aptitude for rapidly learning new skills, and she told him so, to his somewhat embarrassed pleasure.

Both were able to outwardly ignore the enforced physical intimacy of dancing during the evening, even when Mallory accidentally brushed against him to discover that he was not completely unaware of the proximity of their bodies. His arousal fueled her own, making it even harder to pretend that nothing was happening between them, but somehow she managed.

And then it was time for him to go.

Mallory walked Elliott to the door, telling him she'd see him at work the next morning.

"I suppose tomorrow night will have to be our last dancing lesson," Elliott commented, pausing at the door before leaving.

She nodded. "Yes. But don't worry. You're going to do great at your grandparents' party. You're a natural dancer."

"And *you* are a very skillful flatterer," he countered with a smile, touching a finger to her cheek. "But thanks, anyway."

She laughed. "Tomorrow night we'll practice rock and roll—just in case your grandparents decide to get down and get funky at their bash."

He grinned. "Sure. And then they'll invite everyone to join them in a game of strip canasta. My grandparents wouldn't know how to 'get down and get funky' if you gave them an instruction manual."

"Still, it never hurts to be prepared," she quipped, loving the way his dark eyes glittered with amusement.

Her smile faded as their gazes locked. The amusement left Elliott's eyes, to be replaced by a hunger that she couldn't misinterpret. He wanted her, she acknowledged with a hard swallow. Just as she wanted him. If only she could believe that their attraction could lead to anything but heartache for her.

She didn't resist when Elliott lowered his head slowly to hers, watching for her reaction as he did so. His lips brushed across hers, once, twice, and then settled firmly as the kiss became a heated, volatile expression of their pent-up emotions.

The embrace lasted a very long time. Mallory was trembling when it ended, and she thought that Elliott was, too. His voice was husky when he spoke. "Good night."

"Good night," she whispered, unable to summon her full voice.

She locked the door behind him and then stood for several long moments with her forehead pressed to its wooden surface, knowing she'd sleep no more that night than she had the night before. Mallory wondered despairingly if it was too late to protect herself from Elliott Fraser, if the heartache was already inevitable. . . .

ELLIOTT GAVE MALLORY a look of quizzical dismay when she placed the needle on the record and a pounding rock and roll tune surged into his living room. "You expect me to dance to *that*?" he asked her skeptically.

She giggled and reached for his hands. "Yep."

He shook his head, the overhead light glinting off his dark red hair. "You're suffering from delusions, sweetheart. There's no way I can ever dance to this."

Mallory was momentarily diverted by the casual endearment, but forced herself to begin his lesson. Fifteen minutes later they were laughing as they stumbled through one dance after another, though occasionally Elliott made a clever move that surprised both of them. By the end of another hour they were actually managing to dance quite creditably together. Looking smugly pleased with himself, Elliott lifted her arm over her head, spinning her into a dramatic conclusion to the number.

The music ended, and Mallory found herself draped backward over Elliott's arm, clinging to his shoulders with both hands. "I'm impressed," she admitted, grinning up at him.

"You should be." And still he made no move to lift her upright.

Mallory cocked a questioning eyebrow. "Are you going to let me up now?"

He appeared to give the question serious consideration. "I'm not sure," he said at last. "I kind of like you in this position. I don't get the upper hand with you

very often." He bent lower, until she was dangling only
a foot or so above the floor.

Laughing, Mallory pushed futilely upward. "The
blood's rushing to my head," she protested.

"You go to my head," he muttered, his face close to
hers.

She went still at the look in his eyes. He wasn't playing now—and neither was she. "Elliott," she murmured, her hands lifting from his shoulders to cup his
face.

Somehow she found herself lying on her back on the
glossy hardwood floor, Elliott on top of her as his
mouth settled forcefully onto hers.

There were no preliminaries this time, no tentative
testing of her response. His tongue pushed demand-
ingly between her teeth, taking the moist sweetness beyond as if by right. Mallory closed her eyes and tilted
her head backward to give him better access, making
no effort to protest his presumption. Her tongue joined
his for a dance in which neither was the teacher, neither the student, but both willing, equal participants.

She shivered when his hand moved from her waist
to settle for the first time onto her right breast. Her
heated flesh swelled to fill his palm, aching for more of
his touch. She'd only imagined his hands on her before; now she discovered reality to be far more arousing than fantasy. Her skin tingled, frustrated by the
layers of cloth separating them, longing to be pressed
to his bare warmth. "Elliott," she whispered again,
tugging at him with eager, hungry hands.

He muttered something incoherent and buried his
face in her throat, his lips moving against her racing

pulse. His hand slipped beneath her loose pullover top, stroking her stomach before moving upward to release her from the confines of her sheer bra. And then his fingers were circling her nipple, tugging gently until she cried out and arched upward, pressing herself more firmly against the hardening length of his body.

Forcing her eyes open, she looked at him through a haze of need, wondering at the difference in him. His tautly drawn skin was flushed, his hair disheveled, his dark eyes glittering with a ferocity she wouldn't have expected from him. And then his head lowered, hiding his expression from her as his mouth hovered only a warm breath away from her distended nipple.

Her hands clenched impatiently in his hair, pulling him down even as she pushed herself up to meet him. She gasped when his mouth settled warmly, wetly over the tip of her breast, his tongue circling, lips tugging until she was half wild with the glorious sensations he drew from her. Her breath was ragged, tortured, punctuated by husky little moans as her legs shifted against his, parting to cradle him between her thighs. His hard arousal pressed into her, throbbing through the fabric of her jeans and his slacks, leaving her in no doubt as to how badly he wanted her. His hips shifted, thrusting almost lazily against her, and she cried out with the near-painful glory of it.

Thought, logic had deserted her. She couldn't remember why she'd wanted to avoid this, couldn't consider the possible consequences. Her thoughts, her senses were filled with Elliott, with the things he was doing to her, the things she wanted to do to him in return. Her hands were insatiable as they swept his back, pausing to clench briefly into his taut, twill-covered buttocks, moving on to stroke his arms and shoulders. His mouth was just as voracious, moving feverishly from one breast to another, then tasting lower with hard, stinging little kisses that led downward to the snap of her jeans.

There he paused, pressing his hot cheek to the glistening skin of her stomach as he fought for control. "We have to stop," he groaned in a voice she would not have recognized as his.

Stop? she repeated in silent dismay. "Elliott, I—it's okay. I'm protected," she whispered, thinking that must be why he hesitated. "I'm on the pill."

He stiffened, then slowly raised himself until their eyes met. "Is this really what you want, Mallory?" he demanded, his gaze boring into her.

Yes! she wanted to shout. She stared at him. "No," she managed at last. "You're right, I was—carried away. I wasn't thinking."

"That goes for both of us," he murmured, pushing himself up to sit beside her. "I'm sorry."

Her hands were shaking so hard that she had a difficult time refastening her bra and adjusting her top. Elliott made no effort to help her, for which she could only be grateful. Breathing deeply to steady herself, she made it to her feet. "Don't apologize. I'm grateful to you for stopping when you did. I've told you all along that I don't want us to confuse our charade for a real situation."

"You don't want an affair with your employer," he quoted her, his hands deep in his pockets as he stood several feet away from her.

"That's right." *I don't want to fall in love with you. And I'm afraid it's already too late.* "I guess I'd better go."

He frowned. "You're okay? For driving, I mean?"

She lifted her chin. "I'm perfectly capable of driving, Elliott."

He nodded. "All right. I'll see you in the morning."

"Yes. Good night."

"Good night."

He made no move to accompany her to the door. She wondered if he still didn't trust himself to let her go. She found herself foolishly wishing he'd call her back. And then she tried to tell herself that she was glad he hadn't as she grimly headed her Ford toward her empty apartment.

6

MALLORY SAW LITTLE of Elliott on Thursday. He spent most of the day at the university—deliberately, she suspected. It took all her concentration to do her work without dwelling on what had taken place between Elliott and her the evening before. She'd had all night to relive that, after all. And she had relived each moment over and over, until she'd finally buried her face in her pillow and somehow forced herself to sleep.

Was Elliott having as difficult a time forgetting? she wondered sometime during the day. Had it been as hard for him to stop the lovemaking as it had been for her? Had he only been thinking of her needs when he'd stopped, or had there been reasons of his own that he'd suddenly drawn away from her?

He finally returned from the university just as she was getting ready to leave for the day. She briskly went over his messages with him, then reached for her purse.

"I'll pick you up at seven-thirty for the reception tonight."

She nodded. "All right." She wasn't looking forward to the function, but she'd promised she'd go with him, and she would not back out now. She only hoped they'd make it through the evening without a repeat of the night before. She wasn't sure she could survive being taken that close to ecstasy again, only to be abruptly dropped back to earth.

She'd have to make very sure they kept their distance. She hoped she had the strength to do so.

ONCE AGAIN, Elliott found himself amazed by Mallory that evening. How could she fit in so easily with a group of strangers? he asked himself, watching her mingling with apparent confidence in the roomful of university faculty and their dates and spouses. He couldn't help but envy her self-confidence in situations that were new to her. She'd dressed conservatively in a simple black dress that highlighted her slender figure without being at all inappropriate for the evening. Her hair was swept up into a sleek roll that made her appear taller, more sophisticated. Discreet jewelry sparkled at her ears and throat. He found it hard to believe this was the same Mallory he knew so well, the woman who preferred oddly-twisted ponytails and baggy khaki clothing.

Until she smiled. And then she was Mallory, her offbeat humor and innate warmth readily apparent. The charm of that smile had not been lost on his associates. Even Elliott had never mixed in as well with his peers as Mallory was doing. If he were a man who believed in the supernatural, he'd swear she was a witch, casting spells over everyone she met.

One man, in particular, seemed especially taken with Mallory during the evening. A professor of economics whom Elliott knew only slightly, Drew Norton was a few years older than Elliott, a few inches shorter, tanned and trim and very popular among the female students. Elliott scowled as he realized just how long Drew had been hovering around Mallory. Abruptly deciding it was time to begin practicing for his role as her lover, he headed grimly across the room, not realizing that he'd ended a conversation with another professor in the middle of a sentence.

The moment he reached her, he draped a possessive arm around Mallory's shoulders, drawing her firmly against him as he nodded rather curtly to the other man. "How are you, Norton?"

The warm smile he'd been wearing dimming visibly, Drew returned the greeting. "Hello, Fraser."

Elliott turned his head toward Mallory, who was looking a bit surprised by his behavior. "I'm sorry I left you for so long, darling. I got trapped by a rather long-winded colleague, I'm afraid. Were you terribly bored?" The wording was deliberate. He didn't miss Mallory's slight wince at his rudeness.

"No, Elliott, I wasn't bored at all," she answered lightly, making an effort to cover for him. "Drew and I were having a very nice chat."

"Still, I won't leave you alone that way again. Forgive me?" he asked in an intimately low tone.

Satisfied that he'd made his point, Elliott turned back to Drew. The two men carried on a brief, superficial conversation for a few more minutes, Elliott's arm never leaving Mallory's shoulders, and then Drew excused himself to drift away, casting one rather wistful look back at Mallory.

"You're overdoing it, Elliott," Mallory hissed the minute they were alone, her bright smile never wavering.

He lifted an eyebrow. "Isn't this the way possessive lovers are supposed to behave?"

"No one said you had to act like a jealous Neanderthal," she muttered, shifting within the confining circle of his arm. "Really, Elliott—"

"Ah, Elliott, there you are." The rotund, bald little man stopped in front of them as he spoke. He wasn't at all what most people expected of the president of a prominent Dallas university, but Elliott had nothing but respect for the older man.

"Dr. Carlson," he greeted him. "Have you met my—um—friend, Mallory Littlefield?"

"Only over the telephone," Carlson replied, taking Mallory's hand in his as he smiled approvingly at her. "She and I have chatted several times when I've called your office during the past few weeks."

"It's very nice to finally meet you in person, Dr. Carlson," Mallory told him with her warmest smile.

Elliott wasn't at all surprised that Carlson succumbed immediately to the magical properties of that smile. Beaming like an aging cherub, he insisted on escorting Mallory to the refreshment table, telling her she really must taste the punch. Elliott followed closely, one eye on Drew Norton, who hovered close by as if waiting for another opportunity to be alone with Elliott's date. Elliott intended to make quite certain no such opportunity arose.

He was jealous, he realized in almost detached surprise. He'd never been jealous of a woman in his life, but it was an emotion he recognized immediately. The primitive, decidedly forceful emotion made him vaguely uncomfortable. It seemed so alien to the man he'd always thought himself to be. But then, he thought, he hadn't quite been himself since he'd first set eyes on Mallory Littlefield. He wondered if his life would ever be the same again. Somehow he doubted that it would.

By the time they left an hour or so later, Elliott was satisfied that he'd made his claim on Mallory quite clear to everyone in attendance at the event—Drew Norton, in particular.

Mallory barely waited until the car doors closed around them before turning to Elliott with a frown. "What in the world were you trying to do tonight?" she demanded.

He hoped the look he gave her was innocent enough. "What do you mean?" he asked, starting the car.

"You did everything but post Off Limits signs on me," she retorted spiritedly, fastening her seat belt with a resounding snap. "If you act that way in Chicago, your family's going to think you've lost your mind."

"Are you saying that my performance was unsatisfactory?" he questioned mildly, guiding the Corvette out of the parking lot.

"It simply wasn't you," she explained with an attempt at patience. "Even if you and I were really involved, it wouldn't cause you to suddenly turn into a possessive, jealous male, Elliott."

Want to bet? he almost asked her, knowing there hadn't been much acting involved in his behavior that evening. He managed to keep his mouth shut.

When she realized he wasn't going to say anything, Mallory continued her lecture. "When we get to Chicago, there's no need to overact to convince your family that you and I are close. Treat me pretty much as you always do, acting as if you care a great deal for me without overemphasizing the point."

Again, he knew he wouldn't be acting. He *did* care for Mallory. More than she wanted to know. He simply wasn't quite sure what he intended to do about it.

Immersed in his own thoughts for the remainder of the drive, he said little. He left Mallory at her door, gently refusing her hesitant invitation to accompany her inside. He thought he saw both disappointment and relief in her eyes when it was apparent that there would be no kisses that evening, no chance for things to get out of hand as they had the night before.

He knew the feeling. Telling her good night, he spun on his heel and left before he could give in to the temptation to say "the hell with it" and haul her off to bed.

IT WASN'T GOING TO WORK, Mallory thought morosely, staring out the airplane window at the distant panorama beneath her. She was going to make a fool of herself. Elliott's family would never believe their charade. By flubbing her part, Mallory would probably ruin his sister's life—and, therefore, Elliott's. She slanted a look toward the man at her side. How could he appear so relaxed, so serene, when he knew what was coming? Didn't he feel guilty about deceiving his grandparents? Heaven knew Mallory did. Didn't he worry about messing up? Mallory was a nervous wreck. So why wasn't Elliott?

He turned to find her looking at him and smiled, his manner so warm and natural that she could almost believe he *was* in love with her. She reminded herself how quickly he'd picked up driving and dancing. A man of his intelligence would be equally adept at learning acting skills, she thought grimly. She'd better keep that in mind during the next few days.

"You didn't tell me you were a nervous flyer," he chided her gently, prying her fingers off the armrest between them and linking them with his. "You look terrified."

"That has nothing to do with the flight," she retorted. "I was just thinking about the coming weekend."

He looked surprised. "You're worried about meeting my family? Don't be. They're very nice people, if a bit conservative in their behavior. I think you'll like them. I know they'll like you."

"Elliott, maybe we shouldn't try this. They'll never believe that we're involved in a hot and heavy love affair."

He lifted her hand to his mouth, brushing her knuckles with his lips as his gaze held hers in a seductive, skin-tingling exchange. "Won't they?" he murmured, his breath warm on the back of her hand.

She gulped. "I think it's possible," she managed in a thin, strained voice, "that I really have created a monster." This was *not* the Elliott Fraser who'd burst into that employment agency three weeks earlier!

He laughed softly and lowered their linked hands to his thigh. "You may just be right, sweetheart."

Mallory swallowed a moan and leaned her head against the back of her seat. Her father had warned her that this trip might be the one situation she'd find she couldn't handle with a joke and a smile.

"You can't go around deceiving a man's family," he'd muttered when Mallory had told her parents about what she and Elliott had planned. "And it isn't always so easy to tell the difference between fantasy and reality when you start playacting, young lady," he'd added sternly.

She should have listened to her father.

ELLIOTT WAS STILL CHUCKLING when he and Mallory deplaned at O'Hare. "Your hand is like ice. Relax, Mallory. It's going to be okay."

She looked up at him with a frown of concern as they stepped into the terminal. "Yes, but what if—"

Ignoring the other passengers shuffling around them, some being noisily greeted with squeals and hugs, Elliott turned to cup Mallory's face between his hands. "Have I told you how much I appreciate your doing this for me?" he asked quietly.

The words calmed her almost magically. She smiled. "I only hope I don't let you down."

"You won't. You couldn't." And then he kissed her with such sweetness, such tenderness that it brought a lump to her throat.

She had *definitely* created a monster, she thought when he slowly released her mouth. But, oh, what a charming monster he had become.

"Elliott?"

The tentative question brought Mallory's head around with a jerk, and she found herself face to face with Elliott's sister.

Sybil was even more beautiful in person than she'd appeared in the photograph in Elliott's office. Her auburn hair, dark eyes, tall, slender body were all displayed to stylish perfection. Mallory swallowed and futilely smoothed at a wrinkle in her full cotton skirt. She found herself being thoroughly scrutinized by those sharply observant dark eyes, so like Elliott's, and she knew it was because Sybil had witnessed that kiss. Elliott's family had been told that he was bringing someone with him for the weekend, but he had been quite vague about the nature of his relationship to Mallory.

It was going to be a very long weekend.

Elliott slipped an arm around Mallory's waist, as if to offer moral support. "Hi, Sybil. Hello, George."

For the first time, Mallory noticed the man behind Elliott's sister. George wasn't a handsome man, but he had the kind of open, pleasant face that made Mallory like him immediately. She thought that perhaps she'd found an ally in Sybil's suitor.

Sybil stepped up to her brother for a kiss, then pulled back and turned to Mallory. "Elliott will probably remember to introduce us eventually, but I think I'll save time and introduce myself. I'm Sybil Fraser. And you must be—"

"Mallory Littlefield," Mallory supplied, taking the cool, slender hand Sybil extended to her. "It's very nice to meet you. Elliott has told me so much about you."

"I wish I could say the same," Sybil murmured with a very expressive look at Elliott.

Elliott only smiled blandly and nodded toward George. "Mallory, this is George Parker."

George shook Mallory's hand with welcoming enthusiasm, grinning at her in a way that reinforced her impression that she and George could be friends. "Nice to meet you, Mallory."

Turning briskly to Elliott, Sybil placed her hand on his arm and pulled slightly. Mallory couldn't help but wonder if she'd deliberately drawn Elliott away from his proximity to Mallory. "We should be going. Elliott, dear, do you have your baggage claim checks? Do you remember where you put them?"

Mallory almost choked at the woman's tone. She was speaking to Elliott as if he were a child! she thought resentfully. And the worst part was that Elliott didn't seem to mind at all.

"Yes, Sybil, I have them," he answered patiently, reaching for his wallet.

Mallory relaxed, her mouth twitching with a smile, when Elliott made quite a show of searching inside his wallet for the papers, flashing his newly-acquired driver's license toward his sister as he did so. Sybil spotted it immediately. "Elliott, that looks like—it's a driver's license!" she exclaimed, catching his arm when he moved to close the wallet.

"Yes, it is," he agreed, flicking Mallory an amused glance.

"But, dear, you don't drive!"

"Oh, but he does," Mallory inserted smoothly, seeming surprised that Sybil didn't already know. "Why he handles his Corvette like a professional driver. I always feel so safe when Elliott drives me," she almost crooned. *So there, Sybil.*

"His Corvette?" Sybil repeated blankly, looking from her brother to Mallory as if both had lost their minds.

"It's new," Elliott explained. "Got it last week. You'd like it, Syb. It's gold and black, low-slung, goes from zero to sixty in just—"

"But when did you learn to drive?" Sybil interrupted.

Elliott smiled and reached out to pull Mallory back to his side. "Mallory taught me. Mallory's taught me a lot of things."

Sybil blinked, cleared her throat and clutched her eelskin handbag a bit more tightly. "Yes, well, we really should be going. Come along." And with that she turned on one high heel and strode briskly off in the direction of the baggage claim area.

Managing not to giggle, Mallory followed at Elliott's side, George tagging along behind them.

She no longer doubted that she was doing the right thing by helping Elliott establish his independence from his family. During the drive to the Fraser home, several things became obvious to Mallory. The first was that Sybil genuinely adored her older brother, though her overprotectiveness of him caused her to treat him with a fond condescension that set Mallory's teeth on edge. The second was that although Sybil and George were very deeply in love, Sybil was still concerned about changing her lifelong habit of being there for her brother.

Mallory shook her head in exasperation as the others carried on a casual conversation in the luxury car. It was well past time that things changed in the Fraser family, she decided firmly, especially if Elliott's grandparents gave him no more credit than his sister did.

It wasn't long before Sybil directed the conversation to Elliott's relationship with Mallory, as Mallory had been expecting. Turning to face them from the front passenger seat, Sybil draped an arm across the back of the seat and smiled politely at Mallory. "Have you and Elliott known each other long?"

"Almost three months," Mallory replied, improvising rapidly.

"We met at a restaurant," Elliott added with an amused glance at Mallory.

"And you never introduced us—or even mentioned her to me," Sybil told her brother, her tone aggrieved.

Elliott managed to look penitent. "I know. I was being selfish, I'm afraid. I wanted to keep Mallory to myself for a while. It was all so new and unexpected, you see."

"Mmm," Sybil murmured noncommittally, still eyeing Mallory with wary curiosity. "Was Gram mistaken, or did you tell her that Mallory is serving as your secretary now?"

"She very graciously agreed to help out while you were gone," Elliott replied innocuously. "It was so much easier for me than hiring a temporary, as you'd suggested. Mallory's an excellent secretary."

"Unemployed at the moment, I take it?"

Mallory nodded equably. "Yes, I was between jobs when Elliott told me that he needed someone to fill in for you." *And you're not getting your job back without a fight*, she thought stubbornly, forgetting for the moment that she'd been considering looking for a new job when she returned to Dallas. Forgetting that Elliott wasn't hers to fight for.

Elliott changed the subject abruptly. "Enough about us. You haven't told me how the cruise went. Did you have a good time?"

Sybil's face softened dramatically as she cast a glowing smile at George. "Oh, we had a wonderful time. The islands were so beautiful—and the sunsets! Breathtaking."

"I'm glad you had a nice time, Syb. You deserved it." Elliott's voice expressed his fondness for his sister, making Mallory's throat tighten as she thought of how wonderful it would be to be loved by Elliott Fraser. "I assume that you and George didn't get tired of each other's company?" Elliott teased.

Sybil flushed delicately. "No, we got along just fine."

George looked into the rearview mirror with a grin. "We found plenty to do to keep us entertained."

Sybil's flush deepened. "George!" she remonstrated, avoiding Mallory's eyes.

The men only laughed as Mallory smiled in sympathy. Surprisingly enough, she was beginning to like Sybil, despite the other woman's rather peremptory manner. She wished she knew what had been decided about Sybil's future with George.

ELLIOTT'S GRANDPARENTS' HOME was dauntingly large and luxurious. Mallory swallowed uneasily, her hand automatically slipping into Elliott's as he turned to assist her from the car. His fingers closed comfortingly around hers, and he gave her a wink of encouragement. They'd hardly gotten out of the car before the double doors at the top of the gleaming steps opened and a petite, lavender-clad figure topped with sleekly styled gray hair rushed out. "Elliott!" the woman greeted, stepping into her grandson's fervent one-armed embrace. "I'm so glad you're here."

"So am I, Gram." He pulled Mallory forward with the hand he hadn't released. "I want you to meet Mallory. Mallory, this is my grandmother, Vivian Fraser."

Where Sybil's eyes had expressed wariness and perhaps even a hint of suspicion at meeting Mallory, Vivian's brown eyes gleamed with what appeared to be sheer delight. "Lovely," she pronounced, taking Mallory's hand and looking her up and down with approval. "How was your flight, dear?"

Mallory felt herself warming to Elliott's grandmother immediately. "It was fine, thank you, Mrs. Fraser."

Vivian slipped her hand under Mallory's arm. "I'm sure you'd like to freshen up. I'll show you the way to your room."

Mallory looked back toward the car. As if reading her mind, Vivian shook her head, still smiling broadly. "Don't worry about your bags. Kellogg will take care of them."

Kellogg? Before she could ask, Mallory found herself being hustled inside by the surprisingly strong older woman. She threw one last look over her shoulder at Elliott, who was grinning at her in appreciation of her sudden speechlessness.

"This will be your room, dear," Vivian announced a few minutes later, after leading Mallory up a flight of marble stairs that could have come from the set of a glitz movie. "I hope you find it satisfactory."

"It's lovely," Mallory replied weakly, trying to keep her jaw from dropping. The bedroom was roughly the size of her entire apartment in Dallas, furnished in gleaming antiques and delicate lace. She'd dreamed of having a room like that when she was a teenager.

Vivian beamed. "I'm glad you like it." She waved one pale, beringed hand toward a door on one wall. "You'll be sharing a bath with the next bedroom. I hope you don't mind."

"No, of course not. Who's in the next room?"

Vivian giggled, her lined face pinkening. "Why, Elliott, of course."

"Oh." Mallory's voice sounded hollow, even to her. "Of course." She wondered how often Elliott brought women home to this exquisite room, so conveniently connected to his. Had the brilliant Petra tiptoed through that bath in the middle of the night? she questioned, before chiding herself for being such a dolt.

"I'm so pleased that you're here, Mallory. You're the first woman Elliott has ever brought home to meet us. And I know my Elliott—he's quite taken with you. I've never seen him look at anyone else the way he looks at you."

Embarrassed, and yet greatly relieved by Vivian's comments, Mallory managed to murmur a vague response.

Vivian laughed. "I'm sorry, I'm embarrassing you. It's just that I've been worried about Elliott. It's not natural for a young man to spend all his time in that isolated intellectual tower of his. I think you'll draw him out into the real world at times. I never knew how. I was always so intimidated by that terribly impressive brain of his."

Mallory fell in love with Elliott's grandmother on the spot. And she felt even guiltier at deceiving the charming woman, who so obviously loved her grandson deeply, despite her admitted awe of him. "Mrs. Fraser, I—"

Whatever confession she would have made was broken off when the other woman immediately shook her head. "No, no. Please call me Vivian. Mrs. Fraser is much too formal. Now I'll go and let you freshen up. Your bags will be up in a moment." Already at the door, Vivian turned to her guest and gave her one last smile. "Oh, and dear?"

"Yes, Vivian?"

"Don't let Sybil upset you. It's only natural that she'll be a bit jealous of you at first."

"Jealous?" Mallory repeated slowly, stunned at the very suggestion that the beautiful, competent Sybil could be in the least jealous of Mallory. "Of me?"

"Of course. Elliott has depended on her for so long, you see. I've always known it wouldn't be easy for Sybil to accept another woman in her brother's life, even though we're all hoping that she and George will start their own family soon. But I believe she likes you, so be patient with her, will you?"

"I—of course." Still dazed, Mallory waited until Vivian had flitted out of the room before sinking into a tiny, chintz-covered chair.

Elliott's voice was richly amused when he spoke from the doorway a few moments later. "Shell-shocked, darling?"

Return this card **TODAY** to qualify for the $1,000,000.00 Grand Prize **PLUS** a Cadillac Coupe de Ville **AND** over 5000 other cash prizes!

If offer card is missing, write to: Harlequin Reader Service® 901 Fuhrmann Blvd P.O. Box 1867 Buffalo NY 14269-1867

Mallory looked up with a scowl, then deliberately bit back her retort when she realized Elliott wasn't alone. It was all she could do not to giggle at her first sight of Kellogg.

The man who carried Mallory's bags into the room was as formally dignified as Mallory would have expected from the butler of a wealthy, prominent family. Holding himself stiffly erect, he stepped briskly into the room and deposited the two slightly battered cases on the floor at the foot of the bed. He was dressed quite appropriately in a dark suit, creased to perfection, and a blindingly white shirt.

And he still looked like a prize-fighter.

Leather-brown and liberally creased, his face was humorously flat, his nose having been broken so many times over the years that it retained very little of its natural shape. His eyes were steel gray and penetrating, the left partially covered by a drooping eyelid. His thin dark hair was slicked back to end just beneath conspicuously distended ears. His crisp shirt collar completely covered the excuse for a neck that separated those ears from his massive shoulders.

"Mallory, this is Kellogg, my grandparents' butler," Elliott said.

Kellogg bowed stiffly from his thick middle. "How do you do, mum," he offered in a low, gravelly Bronx growl.

Mallory smiled broadly at him. "Hello, Kellogg. It's very nice to meet you."

The man's thin lips twitched with the beginnings of an answering smile, swiftly suppressed. "Thank you, mum. You will, of course, let me know if there is anything at all you need."

"Yes, of course." Mallory couldn't help darting one quick, laughing glance at Elliott, who was enjoying her amusement.

"That will be all, Kellogg," he murmured, his expression quite sober, though his dark eyes glittered.

Again, Kellogg bowed. "Thank you, sir."

"Oh, Elliott, he's wonderful!" Mallory exclaimed when they were alone. "Where on earth did your grandparents find him?"

"They advertised for a butler when the last one retired some ten years ago. Gram took one look at Kellogg and hired him on the spot. Grandad wasn't quite as easily won over. He thought Gram had gone temporarily insane. But Kellogg got to him, too, in a matter of days. The man is fiercely loyal and almost rabidly efficient at his job."

"Did he—was his résumé impressive?" Mallory couldn't resist asking.

Elliott grinned. "He was one of the all-time worst boxers in history before he attended a school for menservants, which he confessed had always been his dream. This was his first job in that particular line of work."

"I love it," Mallory enthused, laughing and shaking her head.

"And *I'm* glad you're finally laughing again," Elliott remarked, sitting on the end of her bed, which was only a couple of feet from the chair in which she sat. "I've never seen you as nervous as you were when we arrived."

"I'm still nervous," Mallory admitted. "And I feel so guilty. Your grandmother is a lovely woman, Elliott. Not at all what I'd expected. I hate deceiving her."

Ignoring the last part, Elliott cocked his head and asked, "What *did* you expect?"

Mallory shrugged. "Someone rather stern and humorless, very conscious of social position, perhaps even a bit snobbish. She's not at all that way, of course," she hastened to add.

"No," Elliott agreed equably. "My grandfather is, though. You've just described him to a T."

Mallory groaned and hid her face in her hands.

Elliott laughed. "Don't worry about it, sweetheart. You'll charm my grandfather just as you have everyone else."

"Your sister didn't seem particularly charmed," Mallory muttered, lifting her head.

"Oh, Sybil will come around. She's just miffed at the thought that I began a romance without asking her to approve and organize it first."

"She loves you, Elliott."

His face softened. "I know. I love her, too. Which is why I want her to be happy. And I think George will make her happy."

"You'll miss her though, won't you?"

He looked at Mallory for a long time before answering. "I'll miss her," he said at last. "But not as badly as I once might have. Not as badly as I'd miss—"

He stopped abruptly and shoved himself to his feet. "You're probably tired. I'll let you rest awhile before dinner, which is always at six-thirty. My grandparents turn in early when they have no outside plans. Do you want some help unpacking? I can call the maid."

The maid? "No, don't do that. I'll manage just fine."

Elliott smiled. "Somehow I knew you'd say that. See you later."

After Elliott left, Mallory spent several minutes wondering about the sentence he'd left unfinished. *"Not as badly as I'd miss—"* Who? Me?

Mallory swallowed, wondering if she were the only one having trouble separating their charade from reality. She knew how hard it would be to resist Elliott if he made the mistake of confusing the two, as well.

7

ELLIOTT HADN'T EXAGGERATED about his grandfather.
Gyles Fraser, though scrupulously polite, was not exactly warm and outgoing. He seemed quite fond of Elliott and Sybil, in a rather detached way. But his no-
nonsense manner was just what Mallory would have
expected from the man who hadn't encouraged Elliott
to learn to drive because he'd wanted him to utilize
travel time working and studying.

He also seemed particularly concerned about Mallory's role in his grandson's life. Several remarks he
made during dinner led Mallory to wonder in annoyance if Gyles actually believed that being in love would
make Elliott any less brilliant, any less successful in his
field. Honestly, she thought, making an effort not to
glare at the man.

Though Mallory noticed nothing unusual in Elliott's
behavior during the evening—he teased and laughed
with her as easily as he always had—his family seemed
surprised by his good humor. She wondered how he
normally behaved with his family. Probably exactly the
way they expected, she thought. Like some sort of ste-
reotype of a withdrawn, absentminded professor/ge-
nius. Poor Elliott.

"I think your grandfather suspects that I'm a gold
digger."

Elliott chuckled and slipped his arm around Mallory's waist as they walked by the pool later that night. As Elliott had predicted, the elder Frasers had turned in quite early, followed soon afterward by Sybil and George. Left to themselves, Mallory and Elliott had wandered outside to enjoy the fragrant late-summer evening in the beautifully landscaped back garden. "A gold digger, huh? You think Grandad finds it so inconceivable that you may be genuinely attracted to me?"

"I think he's wondering, instead, what *you* see in *me*," she answered honestly.

Elliott's arm tightened, pulling her closer to his side. "I could tell him, if he asked. In great detail."

Mallory flushed, grateful for the shadows that hid her pink cheeks from him. "Behave yourself."

"Haven't I been behaving quite properly this evening?" he asked, sounding aggrieved. "I've been attentive and considerate without overplaying my role, as you accused me of doing at the faculty reception. I haven't embarrassed you with any suggestive remarks in front of my family. *I* think I've been the perfect example of a man in love with a beautiful, fascinating woman."

Mallory's cheeks flamed several degrees hotter. "Come off it. We both know I'm not beautiful."

"Yours isn't a classic perfection of features, perhaps," Elliott agreed. "But beauty can be defined in many ways. In a pair of clear green eyes that gleam with a contagious enthusiasm for life. In a warm, generous smile that defies anyone to see it and not smile in return. In a pert little nose dusted with freckles begging to be counted, one by one. In shining red hair shot with strands of gold and a slender, healthy body that makes a man's hands itch to caress it."

Mallory stopped walking long before Elliott finished speaking, turning to stare at him with an unromantically slackened jaw as her kneecaps slowly disintegrated. She reached out blindly to place her hand on a low brick wall, steadying herself. "Elliott," she pleaded hoarsely, not quite sure what she was asking of him. Knowing her chances of resisting him were getting slimmer with each moment she spent with him.

"You are beautiful, Mallory," he continued inexorably, turning to trap her against that low wall. "Beautiful and so very, very fascinating."

His lips covered hers before she could voice another protest.

The faint moan she'd meant as reproach sounded suspiciously like one of pleasure. Surrendering to the inevitable, she didn't even try to resist further. Closing her eyes, she wrapped her arms around his waist and opened her mouth to his.

Elliott murmured his approval of her surrender, his mouth softening on hers, caressing her with the skill he'd refined over the past few weeks. His hands claimed her curves with a possessive hunger he made no effort to disguise. Mallory melted against him, tingling everywhere he touched—which included most of her body by the time the long, ardent kiss ended.

Making a massive effort to refrain from panting, Mallory pulled away from him, swallowing hard. "We'd better go in," she managed in a voice that sounded as if it had been sandpapered.

Looking more than a bit dazed, Elliott nodded mutely. He very obviously avoided touching her as they walked side by side into the house and up the stairs to their all-too-close bedrooms. Their good-nights were muttered without looking at each other, and then they each escaped into the privacy of their rooms.

MUTTERING A CURSE she hadn't used in years, Mallory savagely punched her pillow and burrowed into it, trying to force herself to sleep. It wasn't easy, knowing that Elliott was in the next room. She kept thinking of how simple it would be to walk through the connecting bathroom and crawl into the bed beside him.

"Stupid, stupid, stupid," she groaned softly, rapidly fanning her face with her hand. She'd just been congratulating herself a few minutes earlier for not allowing that kiss by the pool to escalate into anything more, and now all she could think of was Elliott's tall, lean body, lying warm and willing between soft, welcoming sheets.

"You're an idiot, Littlefield."

It hadn't been easy to pull away from him earlier. The kiss had been spectacular, particularly after his uncharacteristic and wholly unexpected flight into poetic tribute to her alleged beauty. He'd really caught her off guard that time.

She could easily slide into love with Elliott Fraser, if she hadn't been foolish enough to do so already.

She tried to remember what it had been like when she'd thought herself in love with Larry. Not like this. It had been exciting, exhilarating, fun—but it hadn't been terrifying. It hadn't been so close to painful that she ached with the power of it. She hadn't been devastated when it ended—only angry and chagrined and embarrassed at allowing herself to be used that way.

But being with Elliott for only a short time, and then having to give him up—well, she wasn't sure *devastated* fully described the way she'd feel if that were to happen. And, for the first time in her reckless, adventurous life, Mallory Littlefield was afraid. Deeply afraid.

"WHAT HAVE YOU DONE to Elliott?"

Mallory was astonished at Vivian's question. "I'm not sure what you mean."

Vivian waved an expressive hand across the crowded ballroom to where her grandson stood in apparently innocuous conversation with several older men. "My dear, he's actually making *small talk*! Why, only a few months ago he would have been perfectly miserable at this anniversary party, standing in a corner sulking about having to be here at all. Tonight he has mingled like a man who's having a very pleasant evening, enjoying the chance to socialize. This must be your doing."

"Well, I have encouraged him to make more of an effort to mix with people in social gatherings, but I certainly didn't coach him on what to say or do," Mallory explained, again feeling that strange defensiveness for Elliott. "His main problem with this sort of thing in the past was that he's rather shy. He's simply learning to overcome it."

Vivian blinked. "Elliott? Shy?"

"Yes," Mallory confirmed, beginning to smile. "Shy. He's always been afraid that he would bore people with his conversation, so he's remained quiet because of that fear—unless, of course, he was with a group of his peers in science or education. I hope I've managed to convince him that he is a witty, articulate man who has a great deal to contribute to any gathering."

Shaking her stylish gray head, Vivian peered fondly at Mallory through her somewhat myopic eyes. "In such a short time, you've accomplished what I've been trying to do for years. I'm very grateful to you, dear. Elliott has seemed to relaxed, so happy this weekend. I've always hoped he would find someone like you, someone who would see him as more than a brilliant mind or a sizeable bank account."

Mallory almost squirmed with guilt. "Um, Vivian—"

She was interrupted when Elliott joined them, smiling at his grandmother before turning to Mallory. "We haven't danced all evening," he reminded her, holding out his hand. "Shall we?"

Vivian clapped her hands together in apparent ecstasy. "He dances, too?"

Elliott only chuckled as Mallory placed her hand in his. "Weren't you the one who insisted I learn the steps, Gram?"

"Yes, but you refused to practice and you were terrible," Vivian replied bluntly. "I certainly hope you've improved, since you're risking this wonderful young woman's toes by taking her out on the floor."

"Now would I do anything to harm those beautiful toes?" Elliott chided, glancing down at Mallory's feet in their skimpy dancing sandals. Her toes promptly curled under in acute embarrassment at having such attention called to them. He grinned back up at her flushed face. "Come, sweetheart, let's show Gram what a talented grandson she has."

They had hardly begun to dance before Mallory glared up at him. "I hope you feel like a heel. *I* certainly do!"

"Why?" he asked, looking innocently surprised.

"Dammit, Elliott, your grandmother is almost prepared to build a shrine in my honor! You should be ashamed of yourself for hiding the real you from your family for so long."

"I never deliberately hid the real me from my family," he denied immediately. "I simply didn't know how to relax and be myself until you showed me."

"Now, don't you start, too," Mallory warned in exasperation. "I haven't done anything you couldn't have done yourself."

"You've taught me to drive, to dance, how to act at a party. You've made a great many changes in my life, Mallory Littlefield."

"Changes you wouldn't have made, regardless, had you not been ready to do so," she retorted. "You were the one who changed, Elliott. I simply provided a practice partner."

"I think we'd better agree to disagree on this one." He pulled her closer, smiling down at her. "You're very beautiful tonight, Mallory. Have I told you yet?"

He always seemed to know exactly what to say to make her forget what she'd been talking about. Mallory cleared her suddenly tight throat and turned her eyes downward, focusing on a spot somewhere in the middle of his left shoulder. "Thank you."

Recklessly dipping into her second paycheck from Elliott, Mallory had purchased her dress especially for this party, and she knew it had been an excellent choice. The ivory fabric clung to her breasts and the tops of her hips, swirling around her legs when she walked or danced. Her throat and shoulders were bare, and her waist was emphasized by a slim belt with a flirty, sparkling buckle. She'd fallen in love with the dress at first sight and probably would have bought it even if it hadn't been on sale—though she wasn't sure how she would have paid for it. Now she felt as if the dress had been worth any amount of sacrifice, just to have Elliott look at her in that intoxicating way.

She decided she'd better change the subject while she was still coherent, before she made a fool of herself in front of Elliott's family and friends. "Are you having a nice time tonight?"

"Yes, surprisingly enough. It's funny. . . ." he mused.

"What's funny?" she prodded when he hesitated.

He shrugged slightly. "My grandparents' friends seem to be treating me differently this evening. More normally. Usually everyone is so deferential, almost, when they talk to me. As if they were intimidated by me, or something. Am I making sense?"

It was all she could do not to pull him into her arms for a hug. "Yes, Elliott, you're making sense," she managed steadily enough. "Has it occurred to you yet that the other guests are treating you more casually because you're so much more relaxed than usual this evening? If I'd met you at a social function such as this one, and you'd behaved as you did at the party my friends gave, you'd certainly have intimidated me. I wouldn't have known what to say to you, afraid that you'd find anything I might have to say silly or inconsequential."

He cocked his head at that, staring down at her in surprise. "You? But you've never treated me any differently than you do anyone else. I've never seen you act the least intimidated—even that first week of working for me, when I was behaving abominably."

She couldn't help but laugh softly. "Elliott, you and I hardly met under normal circumstances, remember? We'd already established a pattern of behavior by the time I learned that I was supposed to be in such awe of you."

Smiling at her teasing, he lowered his voice—and his head. "Then I'm glad we met the way we did," he murmured, just before brushing her lips with his. "Very glad."

Her knees went weak at his infinitely gentle caress. She sagged bonelessly against his chest, grateful for the support of his arms around her. "You really should stop doing that," she told him somewhat hoarsely, aware of the interested looks they were receiving from his grandparents' guests—not to mention his family.

"Probably," he agreed equably, then kissed her again to show her that he didn't always do what he should.

It's an act, Mallory told herself desperately, finishing the dance in silence. *It's all just an act.*

But she knew, even as she thought the words, that for her at least, the charade had ended before it had even begun. There was nothing feigned about her feelings for Elliott.

IT WAS VERY LATE when Elliott finally walked Mallory to her door that night. Casting a quick, reluctant look at his own room next door, he turned to her with a visibly strained smile. "I suppose you're tired."

She was, actually, but she wasn't at all sleepy. She didn't mention that particular fact. "Yes, I am. It was a very nice evening, Elliott."

He nodded. "My grandmother seemed quite pleased with her party, didn't she?"

"Yes, she did." Knowing she should bolt into her room and lock the door before she did something she was sure to regret, Mallory still hesitated. "Did—um—did you talk to George during the evening? How's he doing with Sybil?"

"He seems very pleased with the progress they're making, though he hasn't said anything specific. However, Sybil did say that she'd like to speak to me alone in the morning."

"That could be good news. Maybe she wants to tell you that she won't be returning to her job."

"Could be," he agreed. He glanced wistfully into her room through the open door before looking back down at her. "Guess I'd better turn in. Good night, Mallory."

"Good night, Elliott." She waited just long enough to realize that he wasn't going to kiss her before slipping into her room and closing the door behind her. She didn't lock it, but instead stood gazing longingly at it, unreasonably disappointed that there had been no test of her willpower that evening.

ELLIOTT UNDRESSED slowly, draping his clothing haphazardly over a chair as he stared morosely at the doorway to the bathroom that connected him with Mallory's room. He hadn't even trusted himself to kiss her good-night, knowing it would take only that for him to sweep her into his arms and carry her to bed despite her objections. He was determined not to rush her, not to push her into something she didn't want—an affair with her boss. He knew how she felt about it, she'd told him often enough, and he owed her his respect for her wishes.

But, God, he wanted her.

He didn't expect to sleep a wink that night.

COLD WATER.

Mallory stopped her restless pacing as the words slipped into her mind. Her eyes turned toward the bathroom door, her thoughts to the man beyond who'd told her good-night only an hour or so earlier. She didn't want to risk a cold shower for fear of disturbing him, but she could risk washing her face in cold water, she decided, heading toward that door. She didn't really expect it to help all that much, but she had to try something.

She didn't stop to put on her robe. There had been nothing but silence from Elliott's room since they'd parted. She assumed he was already sleeping, and she envied him.

Absorbed in her own thoughts, she opened the bathroom door—only to stop short at the sight of Elliott standing at the sink, his hand on the round brass knob that would turn on the cold water. Obviously they'd had the same idea.

Wearing nothing but the bottom to a pair of pajamas, he looked wonderful in the dim glow of an amber night-light. She'd never seem him without a shirt. His chest was leanly muscled, sparsely covered with dark red hair, tapering down to a flat stomach and narrow hips above his long, straight legs.

She began to tremble as she stared at him, her voice lost somewhere behind the golfball-sized lump in her throat.

Moving only his eyes, Elliott studied her hungrily. She was so lovely. He'd never seen her hair down. It rippled in a cinnamon-red cloud to her shoulders, soft and inviting, making him ache to bury his face in it. She'd washed off her party makeup, and her skin glowed with health and natural beauty, the dusting of freckles only tempting him to explore them more closely. Her eyes were glowing, smoldering with banked flames that mimicked the fires burning deep in his loins. She was wearing a nightgown of midnight blue satin and lace, covering but not concealing her charms.

He couldn't speak.

Long moments passed as they looked at each other, motionless. And then Mallory cleared her throat and managed a weak apology for walking in on him. The voice was hers, yet strangely unfamiliar to both of them.

Elliott approached her carefully, as if afraid of frightening her away. Mesmerized by the way he looked at her, she didn't—couldn't—move.

As if in slow motion, his hands rose to frame her face. "I want you," he told her roughly. "I have never wanted anyone the way I want you now."

She swallowed hard, her trembling accelerating until she wondered dimly if her legs would continue to support her. The truth tumbled from her unsteady lips before she could even think of holding it back. "I want you, too. Oh, Elliott—"

It had been her one chance to pull back. Elliott allowed her no second opportunity. His mouth came down on hers, hard, almost rough in its fiery possession. She could do nothing more than cling to him, lost in the flames he fanned within her.

His hands were as insatiable as his mouth. They swept her body, stroking over satin and lace to trace the slender curves beneath. Rediscovering places he'd explored before, hungrily learning new ones. Her breath coming in soft, strangled moans, she arched against him, her own hands clenching into the warm skin of his shoulders as she struggled to remain upright.

And then the nightgown was gone, pooled around her feet, and she stood before him in nothing but tiny bikini panties. "Mallory," he groaned, eyes and fingertips exploring her. "You're so very beautiful."

"Please, Elliott," she whispered, stroking his chest with shaking hands. "You're making me crazy. I can't take much more of this."

"Oh, yes, you can. Much more," he promised, impulsively sweeping her into his arms and striding toward her bed.

She wouldn't have expected him to carry her to bed. She adored it that he did. Pressing her lips to the juncture of his neck and shoulder, she allowed herself to acknowledge that she and Elliott were going to make love. That she wanted this as she'd wanted nothing before in her life. The decision made, she gave herself up to the pleasure of it, her tongue slipping out to taste him as he lowered her to the bed.

"Your mouth drives me insane," he muttered, tangling his fingers into her hair as she lay back against the pillows and leaning half over her. "I can't seem to get enough of it."

She moistened her lips and smiled, lifting her face to his. "Kiss me again, Elliott. Because I can't get enough of you, either."

Muttering something unintelligible, he smothered her mouth beneath his. He didn't deepen the kiss right away, but rocked his lips slowly over hers, tasting, testing, exploring the differences in textures and angles. He pressed hard, then drew back to nibble, then ran the very tip of his tongue over every inch of her wet, swelling lips before taking them again.

She'd never been kissed with such painstaking care, such obvious enjoyment. Elliott explored her mouth as if he could happily spend hours doing no more than that, as if he'd discovered something wonderful and delicious that he wanted to savor, to linger over for as long as possible. His pleasure in the act increased her own, her hands clenching in his thick hair as she grew hungrier for him to deepen the kiss. She wanted that penetration with a desperation that astonished her, wanted his tongue deep inside her mouth until she couldn't breathe, couldn't even moan, but could only return the caress with everything she had.

When it seemed as though he would never oblige her, Mallory turned aggressive, her hands pulling his head down more firmly to hers, her lips parting, tongue darting between his teeth to tempt his. Elliott chuckled, a low, hoarse sound from deep in his chest, and she realized in amazement that he'd been waiting for just that reaction, teasing her until she'd demanded satisfaction. She ran her short, rounded nails down his shoulders just as his tongue thrust forward, but the small punishment seemed only to incite him further. He kissed her until she was dizzy with it, until pink and yellow lights danced behind her closed eyelids, making her wonder if she'd pass out before she'd ever get her fill of being kissed by him.

And then his mouth moved downward, his hands upward and he was holding her breasts, licking and nibbling and sucking until she writhed helplessly beneath him, her breath coming in sobbing moans, his name tumbling inarticulately from her swollen lips. Her nipples hardened to near painful points of pleasure, the drawing, tugging sensations echoing deep, deep inside her as he paid fervent, thorough homage to first one breast, then the other.

Her legs shifted restlessly, and she felt him against her, hard, quivering, so powerfully aroused. She undulated mindlessly against the hard ridge of his manhood until he gasped her name, one hand going down to clench forcefully on her hip, holding her still. "Don't," he muttered, his voice strained. "I want this to last."

"I want you," she whispered rawly, struggling against his restraint. "Oh, Elliott, I need you. Now."

Shuddering with the force of the control he exerted, Elliott lifted his head and stared down at her. Illuminated only by the soft light coming from the open bathroom door, she glistened palely, her breasts heaving, her hair wildly tumbled. She'd never looked more beautiful. No one had ever looked more beautiful.

And she wanted him. Her skin was hot, damp with the ardor of her desire. He placed a hand on her stomach and felt her flinch in instinctive reaction. No one had ever wanted him so much.

Intoxicated with the power she'd given him, he almost growled in masculine triumph, his hand sweeping downward to divest her of the only tiny garment still covering her. His pajama bottoms followed and then they were both nude; hot, damp skin pressed to hot, damp skin. Their groans of pleasure were perfectly synchronized, as were their heartbeats, their breathing, their very thoughts.

He moved against her thigh, stroking her satin skin with his swollen flesh, half delirious with the feel of her. She cried out softly at his movement, her hips lifting as she sought him.

"Not yet," he whispered, knowing it would be over too soon if he gave in to her silent plea. "Not yet, sweetheart."

Her moan of frustration turned into a cry of delight as his fingers slid into the damply curling cinnamon hair between her thighs. She closed tightly, pulsingly around him when he explored more deeply, moving rhythmically against his hand as he took her mouth once again. The sounds she made as he stroked her were muffled within their kiss, but each one reverberated deeply within him, urging him on.

And then she arched wildly upward, her body convulsing against him. Fragile control shattered, Elliott surged forward, joining their bodies before her shudders stilled, thrusting hard and fast until she was clinging to him again, begging wordlessly for him to end the pleasure that was so intense it hovered too near pain.

This time when she climaxed he was with her, his mind filled with nothing but the feel of her as he exploded in the most shattering release of his experience. Her name was the only sound he was capable of making.

"Mallory, Mallory, Mallory," he chanted hoarsely. "Mallory!"

Even when the power of speech left him completely, when he collapsed onto her, too weak to move, there was only one word in his thoughts, one name sounding endlessly through his mind and echoing in his heart.

Mallory.

8

"ELLIOTT? Elliott, you're crushing me," Mallory murmured regretfully, wriggling beneath him a long, long time later. Had she been able to breathe, she'd have been perfectly content to lie beneath him forever.

He stirred on top of her, then shifted his weight until he lay by her side, reluctantly separating their bodies. "Sorry, sweetheart," he said, making a place for her head on his shoulder as his arms closed warmly around her. "I wasn't thinking clearly."

She laughed softly and snuggled deeper into his still-damp flesh. "That's okay. I'm feeling a bit disoriented myself."

"You're not—" He stopped to clear his throat. "You're not sorry, are you?"

The genuine apprehension in his voice made her hold him tighter and answer immediately. "No, Elliott, I'm not sorry. It was so special, so beautiful. How could I possibly regret what happened between us?"

He relaxed perceptibly. "I'm glad," he said simply.

She lay still as he stroked her hair, her eyelids growing heavy. She was very close to sleep when he spoke again. "Mallory, did you mean it?"

"Mean what, Elliott?" she asked huskily, forcing her eyes open.

"That it was special—beautiful."

He was so insecure, so vulnerable. Her heart twisted painfully. "I meant it."

"It was that way for me, too. I've never—nothing before has ever—" He stopped, seemingly disgusted with the limitations of mere words. "I can't believe I'm about to use that old cliché, but it's all I can think of. I've never felt like that before, Mallory."

She smiled and dropped a kiss on his chest. "Neither have I."

"I've wanted you from the first day. Did you know that?"

She made no effort to be coy. "Yes. I wanted you, too. The attraction was mutual, from the beginning."

"You didn't want this to happen."

"I was afraid."

"Are you still?"

She thought about it a moment. "Yes," she answered finally, honestly. She was even more afraid now. Even more afraid of losing him. Of loving him. Knowing it was too late to protect herself. Much too late.

"I was afraid, too, you know."

"Of what?" she asked, frowning curiously. Could he have been concerned about the same things as she, she wondered on a glimmer of hope. Was he going to tell her that he'd fallen in love, too, and had been just as worried about the risk?

His voice was rather sheepish when he replied. "I was afraid I wouldn't please you. That I wouldn't be passionate enough for you," he admitted hesitantly.

Though it wasn't at all what she'd wanted to hear, she couldn't help but laugh. "Oh, Elliott, you idiot," she murmured fondly, stroking his chest with one lazy hand.

"Does that mean you were satisfied?" he asked, much too casually for her to believe that her answer didn't matter very much to him.

She lifted her head, turning her face to smile chidingly at him. "Elliott, darling Elliott, look at me, will you? My bones have disintegrated, I'm a quivering mass of exhausted flesh. I couldn't move from this bed if the comforter was on fire. Does that sort of hint to you that you were passionate enough?"

He chuckled and hugged her tightly. "You do incredible things to my ego, Mallory Littlefield."

An ego that had been badly, if unintentionally, bruised so often during the years, Mallory added silently, twining her fingertips through the crisp curls on his chest. Who would have believed that a man of Elliott's reputation, a man with all his successes behind him at such a young age, could have been so troubled by so many insecurities, so many doubts?

She shifted more comfortably against him, her leg draped over his, and felt him drop a kiss on her hair. She smiled sleepily, but then her smile faded as she wondered what he was thinking, what he was imagining had just happened between them. Was he feeling some sort of gratitude to her, mistaking that for a more serious emotion? Had he been so ready for changes in his life that he'd given in to an infatuation for a woman who was so totally different from those he'd known before? Neither possibility offered her any pleasure. Gratitude and infatuation were both fleeting emotions, both dissipating so easily in the light of reality.

Her feelings for Elliott weren't at all ephemeral, nor was she in any danger of mistaking them for anything else. She was in love with him. And, in loving him, she'd opened herself to the risk of pain such as she'd never known before. She'd foolishly allowed herself to fall in love with a genius, and she wondered if she could even begin to fulfill this man's special needs.

She wasn't really aware that her wandering hand had drifted lower onto his body until she brushed against his stirring, hardening manhood. Only then did she realize that he was becoming aroused again. Weariness vanishing as if by magic, her body reacted immediately to his desire. "Elliott?" she murmured, her hand closing over him.

He moaned softly, then managed a shaky smile. "You know how it is with scientists," he told her, lifting his hand to stroke one soft, still-tender breast.

Fingertips tactilely measuring his growing interest, Mallory pressed a kiss to one flat male nipple. "How is it with scientists?" she asked huskily.

"We're driven by a compulsion to experiment," he replied, his voice growing rough. "To study all the variables, control conditions, find out if the same results can be obtained more than once."

"That's quite fascinating," she whispered, sliding onto his chest to move sinuously against him. She loved watching his eyes go black with need, his skin tighten over his cheekbones, his mouth grow soft and sensuous. She wondered if she'd ever get enough of watching him while they made love. Her hips rotated slowly, pressing firmly against his groin. "Would a new position be a valid variable in this experiment of yours?"

"Yes," he croaked, his fingers sliding down to grasp her hips. "That would be one interesting variation."

"Then by all means, allow me to assist you in your research, Dr. Fraser," she crooned, taking him into her with one slow, smooth move. Rising above him, her hands at his shoulders, she rocked gently, controlling the pace of their loving until Elliott's breath grew harsh and choppy, his movements more frantic.

Abandoning their teasing, he became abruptly serious, lifting his head to take the tip of one breast into his mouth, worshipping her with lips and tongue and teeth until she arched backward, her hair tumbling around her bare shoulders. As though he'd been waiting only until her control snapped, he shifted suddenly, depositing her beneath him and pressing her down into the mattress as he thrust into her with a desperate, almost savage force that soon had her calling his name in thin, ragged cries.

He pushed her over the edge, miraculously clinging to his own control, waiting until her shudders had subsided before beginning again, driving her toward another incredible release. Helplessly following his lead, Mallory could only hold him, not certain she would survive his passion, not really caring if she did. She was aware of nothing but their writhing, perspiring bodies, their hard, painful breathing, their flaming, all-consuming need. And when the next explosion came, she saw nothing, was conscious of nothing but her name, uttered in a harsh, broken gasp that was the most beautiful sound she'd ever heard.

"Elliott," she breathed, pressing so closely to his hot, heaving body that she couldn't tell where she left off and he began. "Elliott."

ALMOST TREMBLING with the effort, Elliott forced himself through one last lap of the pool, his arms slicing through the water in a steady, relentless rhythm. The early-morning air was cool, the clear water streaked with the colors of reflected sunrise. The house was quiet behind him; he assumed he was the only one awake this early. When he'd slipped from the bed, Mallory had been sleeping deeply, looking so tousled and beautiful that it had been all he could do not to wake her and make love to her again.

Love. The word echoed in his brain in time with the measured strokes of his arms. It had been there all morning, nagging at him, haunting him.

Love. Something he couldn't analyze, couldn't break down into finite, clearly identifiable components. Couldn't manipulate with a change of conditions, a reworking of numbers and statistics. Couldn't study with logical, coolly objective interest in order to understand its properties, its consequences on the future.

He'd never loved a woman, hadn't thought himself capable of the type of love the poets wrote about, musicians sang about. He'd loved his family, his sister, but that love had always been there inside him, something he'd taken for granted, never bothered to examine. It hadn't left him dazed and hurting, wary and apprehensive. He realized now how smug he'd been about his family's love, how arrogantly assured that the emotions would always be there, no matter how badly he acted, how deeply he withdrew into himself. How could he have been so callous about something so precious? And what the hell was he going to do about this new, fragile, overwhelming love he'd discovered for Mallory?

Reaching the end of the pool, he lowered his feet with a gasp of exhaustion, throwing his hair back out of his eyes as he groped for a towel. Someone pressed one into his hand. Blinking rapidly against the water streaming down his face, he opened his eyes to find Sybil crouching beside the pool, looking at him with a smile that was both indulgent and curious. "That was quite an exhibit," she murmured, cupping her chin in her hands. "Just how many laps did you swim?"

"I quit counting after twenty," he answered, planting his palms on the wet tile and lifting himself from the water. Twisting, he sat on the edge, feet still dangling in the pool as he mopped at his head and face with the towel. "What are you doing up so early?"

She reached behind her to pull a delicately ornate metal pool chair closer, settling into it. "I couldn't sleep. When I saw you out here, I thought I'd take advantage of the chance to talk to you alone."

He draped the towel around his neck. "Anything in particular you want to talk about?"

"Several things." She reached out to brush a wet lock of hair off his forehead. "I've missed you, Elliott."

He caught her hand in his and pressed a quick kiss on her knuckles, aware that his gesture of affection had caught her by surprise. He really had been a self-centered jerk with his family, he realized with regret, squeezing her hand before releasing it. "I've missed you, too, Sybil."

She laughed softly, her gaze turning meaningfully to the house. "I think you've managed to keep yourself entertained while I was gone."

Elliott grinned. "Well, yes," he admitted. "But don't tell me that you spent all that time with George missing your brother, either."

Sybil flushed delicately. "Not exactly." She paused only a moment, then asked softly, "Why didn't you tell me about her?"

He found himself incapable of looking her in the eye and lying to her, though he'd had his story all prepared. "I met her the day you left," he confessed.

Her eyes widened in surprise. "But I thought—"

"That I'd known her for several months," he finished, his mouth twisting. "I know. I asked her to say that."

"But why?"

He shrugged. "I wanted you to feel free to go with George, without worrying about me being lonely. It seems silly now that I've said it, but—"

"Oh, Elliott, it doesn't sound silly at all," she assured him, catching his hand in both of hers, not caring that his was still damp. "It was so sweet of you to be concerned about my happiness. And here I was wondering how to tell you that George proposed to me while we were on the cruise, and I accepted."

Now it was his turn to be surprised. "You accepted?" he repeated. "While you were still on the cruise?"

She nodded. "Yes. I was waiting for the right time to tell you, to make sure the news that I'd be moving to

Hawaii wouldn't upset you too badly. Now I see that we've both been very silly."

Elliott laughed and shook his head, thinking that his conspiring with Mallory had been unnecessary, after all. George had been quite capable of pleading his own case, it seemed. And Sybil had given her brother more credit for getting by on his own than either George or Elliott had suspected. But he wasn't sorry that he and Mallory had worked on their elaborate scheme together. How could he be? "When's the wedding?"

"Soon. George begins the new job in six weeks. I'm sure Gram will want the wedding to be held here, but first we have to find a place to live in Hawaii and then spend a few days packing and taking care of everything in Dallas. We'll probably be married here just before we leave permanently for Hawaii."

"I'm very happy for you, Sybil."

Her eyes glowed with unshed tears. "Thank you, Elliott. By the way, I'm going to be pretty busy during the next few weeks. Do you think Mallory would be interested in keeping my job?"

"I think she'd be willing to discuss it," Elliott agreed with a smile.

"I like her, Elliott."

He tilted his head. "You should let her know. She's not sure that you do."

Sybil nodded guiltily. "I know. I wasn't very welcoming to her at first. I guess I was a bit jealous. You'd always turned to me for everything, and then suddenly you were so independent. You had Mallory, and you didn't seem to need me anymore. Even though I knew it was best for both of us, I couldn't help resenting it a little."

"I understand. She does, too. I've explained to her how hard it is to break the habits of a lifetime."

"You're serious about her, aren't you, Elliott?"

He stared at his feet, distorted by the water in which they were submerged. "I think so."

"And you're scared."

He laughed shortly. "Terrified."

Her soft laughter echoed his. "Now that's something I understand completely. It happens to the best of us, brother dear."

He threw her a measuring, sidelong look. "You, too?" It was hard to imagine his competent, efficient, always confident sister having the same doubts and fears he'd been struggling with all morning.

"Of course. Love makes you so vulnerable, so open to pain. I've been so frightened of losing George, of doing something wrong that would destroy everything we've found together. Even now that we've decided to be married and spend the rest of our lives together, I still worry sometimes that I won't make him happy."

"He loves you."

"I know." She beamed with her pleasure in the words. "I love him, too."

"How did you know?" Elliott asked with sudden urgency. "What made you believe that it was real and lasting, that it wouldn't suddenly end?"

"Oh, Elliott, this isn't something you can analyze," Sybil told him fondly, unconsciously repeating his earlier thoughts. "I just knew. People have been trying to understand and explain love since the beginning of time, but it just can't be done. Sometimes people make mistakes, think themselves in love when they're not, or watch their love die for one reason or another. Some people fall in love many times, others only once. I have to believe that the love George and I feel for each other will last for the rest of our lives, whatever trouble or problems we may encounter through the years. I couldn't bear the thought that it might someday end."

Frustrated with the vagueness of her reply, Elliott kicked a spray of water, glumly watching the resulting ripples. He suspected that he was in love with Mallory that way, that he was the once-in-a-lifetime type. But what about Mallory? Did she love him? Maybe she thought she did now, but then she'd admitted that she'd thought herself in love before. What if she changed her mind this time, as she had then? He was terribly afraid that it would destroy him.

"Damn."

Sybil's fingers tightened around his. "Want to talk about it?"

"No," he answered after a pause. "It's too new. I don't know what to say."

"Then do you mind a bit more advice from your bossy little sister?"

He sighed. "I'll take all the advice I can get."

"If you love her, fight for it. You're a man who needs someone to love, someone to share your life, your home. But don't try to change for her. Any changes you make have to come from your own needs, your own desires. Trying to be someone you're not just to please her will only make you both miserable in the end."

He swiveled his head around to look thoughtfully at her. "You think I've been changing to try to please Mallory?"

"No," she answered gently. "I think you've been coming to terms with your own changing needs. You've seemed so much happier, so much more comfortable with yourself this weekend. That's wonderful. All I'm saying is that you can't change the fundamental you. You'll always be different, in some ways, from most people. You're a special man, Elliott, and sometimes those very qualities that make you so special will set you apart from others. If Mallory loves you, she'll understand. She'll learn to accept the times when you turn inside yourself for hours or days, when you lock yourself in your office in a fever of creativity, when you become so absorbed in your work that you forget simple, unimportant things like meals or appointments, birthdays or anniversaries."

"I'm like that, aren't I?" he asked slowly.

"Yes, darling, you are. It's what makes you who and what you are, and you should never regret it, nor try to change it. You're quite capable of making Mallory happy while still being true to yourself. Don't ever doubt that."

Was he? He swallowed hard, wondering if any woman, particularly a happy-go-lucky, adorable impetuous free spirit such as Mallory, could ever learn to live with his eccentricities. Sybil thought so, but then she'd known him all her life. He couldn't quite trust her objectivity where her beloved older brother was concerned. He had so many things to think about before his relationship with Mallory went any further, so many ramifications to consider.

His eyes met his sister's, noting the concern in hers. He smiled. "I love you, Sybil." He couldn't even remember the last time he'd told her.

Her smile trembled. "I love you too, Elliott." She leaned forward to kiss him.

And then she drew back, straightening as she deliberately assumed her usual demeanor. "We really should go in for breakfast now. You need to shower and get dressed. Don't forget that your plane leaves at noon. George and I will drive you to the airport since we're staying on a few days to make plans with Gram about the wedding details. You haven't lost your return tickets, have you?"

"No, Sybil," he replied with assumed meekness. "I haven't lost them." Shoving himself to his feet, he reached out to ruffle her impeccably styled hair in a gesture he hadn't used in years. "See you at breakfast."

FROM HER BEDROOM WINDOW Mallory watched Elliott with his sister. They'd been talking so seriously. She couldn't help but wonder if they'd talked about her.

She'd missed him when she'd awakened, turning instinctively to find him, disappointed that she hadn't had the chance to experience what it was like to wake in his arms. Why had he left her so early?

It was a classic morning after, complete with doubts and insecurities. Smiling wryly at the thought, Mallory ran a hand through her hair. She'd left it down that day for the first time in longer than she could remember, simply because Elliott had seemed to like it so much. She watched as Elliott and Sybil disappeared inside the house, then turned away from the window.

She had just opened her bedroom door when Elliott appeared in the hallway. He'd made an attempt to dry off, but he was still wet, leaving damp, foot-shaped marks behind him on his grandmother's carpet, something which didn't appear to bother him at all. He paused upon spotting Mallory in her doorway. "Oh. Good morning."

Her fingers tightened on the doorjamb at the cautiousness in his greeting. His eyes were shuttered, hiding his feelings from her. He looked so distant. Was he—could he possibly be regretting what had happened between them last night? she asked herself fearfully. Did he, too, realize that there was no basis for them to have a real future together? Was this his way of letting her know?

"Good morning, Elliott."

He shifted his weight, restlessly. "I guess I'd better get dressed," he murmured, gesturing toward his glistening wet skin.

Her eyes followed the movement of his hand, lingering at the narrow black bathing suit that concealed so little. Knowing exactly what was hidden from her, she swallowed, her stomach tightening in the memory of arousal. "Yes, I guess you'd better. Breakfast will be served soon."

He nodded. "I'll meet you downstairs, okay?"

She managed a smile. "Fine."

He hesitated a moment longer, looking as if there were something else he wanted to say—or do—but then he simply nodded and walked away, disappearing into his own bedroom. Mallory's eyes closed in a brief spasm of pain at the awkwardness of their exchange. Why hadn't he kissed her good-morning? Why hadn't he smiled at her the way he'd smiled at her last night? Why was he pulling away from her?

It hurt. Badly.

With little enthusiasm, she took a deep breath and headed toward the dining room.

Sybil and George announced their engagement after breakfast, to the delight of the family. Flushing and glowing with happiness, Sybil accepted her grandparents' hugs and Mallory's congratulations with more warmth than Mallory had seen her display before. Sybil had been treating her quite nicely all morning, actually. She wondered if the talk by the pool with Elliott had made any difference in Sybil's behavior toward her.

She glanced at Elliott, whom she found to be watching her with an almost rueful smile. She smiled back at him, surreptitiously sending him a thumbs-up at the success of their plan. Nodding to acknowledge the gesture, he turned to talk to George.

She was quite sure that no one else in the family had noticed that Elliott was acting at all differently that morning. He'd smiled and teased just as he had all weekend, included Mallory in his conversations and seemed at ease with her. Only she could have known that sometime since last night he'd thrown up an invisible barrier between them, one she doubted that even he thought she perceived. She ached with the confused pain of his withdrawal, but she was determined that no one, not even Elliott, would know. So she smiled, she chatted, she laughed, she even flirted playfully with him as she had all weekend.

And inside, she cried silently.

He knew, of course. Elliott was just as attuned to Mallory as she was to him, and he saw through her laughter to the pain and confusion beneath. He was fully aware that he was the cause of her bewilderment, that she sensed his own concerns about their relationship. He wanted to take her into his arms, to explain that he tended to withdraw into himself when he was confronted by a problem he wasn't sure how to handle. He didn't, of course. What would he have said? That he thought he loved her, but wasn't sure he could make her happy? That he wasn't quite sure how she felt about him, wasn't certain he could trust her to love him without really knowing him for longer than three weeks?

They had to leave soon after breakfast. Elliott watched as Mallory bade a fond farewell to his grandmother, the hug they exchanged touching in its warmth. And then she turned to Gyles, who—as Elliott had predicted—had long since succumbed to Mallory's special charms, and boldly pressed a kiss on the stiffly dignified older man's cheek. It was the first time in his life that Elliott could ever remember seeing his grandfather blush. He shook his head in silent amazement, wondering again if there really was such a thing as witches. She even wrangled a grin and a wink out of Kellogg, with whom she seemed to have formed a lifelong friendship. Was it any wonder that Elliott had been unable to resist her from the first? he asked himself in bemusement.

Sybil and George drove them to the airport. Sybil chattered nonstop the entire way, telling Mallory everything she thought she should know about the job she was relinquishing. Mallory graciously listened to the detailed instructions, asking an occasional question, thanking Sybil for sharing her expertise. If Sybil hadn't already been won over, that ride would have taken care of all her qualms, Elliott decided.

"I'll be seeing you both in Dallas, of course," Sybil informed them as they prepared to board. "We'll be there in a couple of weeks to wrap everything up."

"You'll be very busy preparing to be married and to make such a drastic move," Mallory predicted. "If there's anything I can do to help, give me a call, okay?"

Touched, Sybil nodded. "It's sweet of you to offer. You will be at the wedding, won't you, Mallory?"

Mallory looked at Elliott, who met her eyes blandly. Of course he wanted her with him at his sister's wedding in six weeks. He only hoped that she wouldn't already have grown tired of him and moved on by then. Trying to ignore a sudden feeling of hollowness deep inside him, he managed a smile and answered for her, "I'm going to do everything I can to get her here."

Seemingly satisfied with his response, Sybil kissed her brother's cheek and then Mallory's.

"You told her about us, didn't you?" Mallory asked as soon as the plane had left the runway. "That we weren't—that we haven't really been dating," she explained awkwardly when he cocked an eyebrow in an unspoken request for clarification.

He nodded. "I was tired of pretending," he replied, without thinking about how the words might sound.

Her eyes widened, then her lashed dropped, hiding her expression from him. He sensed immediately that he'd hurt her in some way. Dammit, he thought, tugging impatiently at his seat belt. He hadn't meant to hurt her. He didn't know why he was acting like such a jerk today, but for the life of him he couldn't seem to relax.

He was all wrong for her. She needed someone who could better show her his emotions, who could, at least, understand his own feelings. Elliott felt awkward, confused, at a loss how to even begin to tell her what she meant to him, what last night had meant to him. It was the single most important, most extraordinary event that had ever happened to him, and all he could do was sit around in a funk, worrying about losing her. Wondering if he'd ever really had a chance of holding her.

He swallowed hard and leaned his head back against the seat. Closing his eyes he pretended to doze for the rest of the flight, hoping Mallory would assume he was still tired from the strenuous activities of the night before. He replayed every moment of those activities over and over in his mind until he was forced to deliberately close down his thoughts before he embarrassed both of them. Elliott wanted her again so badly that his hands trembled, and he wished almost desperately that he knew what the hell to do about it.

9

MALLORY HAD SEEN Elliott retreat before, of course. She'd recognized his habit to do so whenever he was feeling threatened or uncertain. But she hadn't expected him to pull back today, not after the night they'd spent together. Not after the closeness she'd thought they shared.

It hurt.

Pretending to read a travel magazine as they sat in silence on the plane, she tried to ignore how near he was sitting. She could almost feel the warmth of his body at her side. She shot him a quick, sideways glance. He sat very still, his eyes closed, looking weary and detached. So very close. And yet he might as well have been miles away.

He must have decided that their lovemaking had been a mistake.

Blinking against incipient tears, she scowled at the magazine, determined not to embarrass both of them by a maudlin display of emotion. Determined not to cry—until she reached the privacy of her own apartment.

She really should have listened to her father.

Back in Dallas, they were on their way to claim their bags when a man's voice called Mallory's name. Turning curiously, she broke into a smile at the sight of the attractive blond signaling for her attention. "David!"

Delighted to see her friend, who'd been out of the country on a career assignment for several months, she stepped into his open arms and returned his enthusiastic hug with warm pleasure. "It's so good to see you," she told him, pulling back to admire his tan. "You look wonderful. When did you get back into town?"

He kissed her on the cheek with a resounding smack. "Fifteen minutes ago," he answered with a grin, his hands still clasping her upper arms. "I planned to call you first thing, but this is even better. How's everyone in the gang?"

"Great. Leslie had her baby last week—a boy."

"Hey, terrific! I'll have to go see him. How's Brock's arm?"

"Much better. He almost has full use of it again. And Debbie . . ." For the next few minutes, they chattered as David caught up on their mutual friends, and Mallory learned as much as she could about his overseas writing assignment with a spate of quick questions. And then she remembered Elliott.

Turning guiltily, she noted that he was more withdrawn than ever, his eyes distant, jaw set in visible impatience. She swallowed, wondering uncomfortably if she'd been deliberately punishing him for ignoring her on the plane. "Elliott, I'd like you to meet one of my best friends, David Garner. David, this is my—my boss, Dr. Elliott Fraser."

Elliott threw her a strange look—one she bemusedly interpreted as a mixture of hurt, censure and a touch of sheer temper—before shuttering his expression and shaking David's hand.

Looking from Elliott to Mallory, David seemed to sense it was time for him to make an exit. "I'll call you, Mal, okay? We'll take in a movie or something and catch up. I've missed you, kid."

"Yes, call me," Mallory urged, hearing the slightest hint of defiance in her own words. Defiance aimed at Elliott. And then she tossed her head and turned to Elliott as David loped off in another direction. "Let's get our bags."

ELLIOTT LEFT MALLORY at her door without going inside. He didn't kiss her when he left, but muttered something about having to hurry home to make some phone calls. She managed to close her door behind her and make it all the way to her couch before bursting into tears of anger and bitter hurt at the way he'd treated her that day. What had she done? she wondered over and over. Why was he so distant when they'd been so very close during the night? Was he confused, maybe a bit scared, as she was, at the intimacy growing so rapidly between them? She could certainly understand that, but why wouldn't he talk to her about it, let her share his concerns? How could he just close her out as he had done?

Because the pain was so deep, she finally allowed the anger to grow, pushing to the forefront. Darned if she'd be the one to try to smooth things over this time, she thought, wiping her eyes rebelliously. Elliott claimed to be fully capable of running his own life; he could start with his love life, if that's what their relationship could be called. It wasn't as if he didn't know how to talk to her. He'd been smooth enough in seducing her, making her want him so badly she'd forgotten all her logical reasons for not getting involved with her employer.

And if he'd decided that Mallory was all wrong for him, if he was trying to come up with an easy way to break the news to her, she'd survive. She'd find yet another job, because, of course, she'd never be able to work for Elliott without remembering and craving the passion they'd shared all too briefly. And she'd never, never forget her hard-learned lessons again. Maybe she'd only work for women from now on.

Not that she'd be in any danger of falling for anyone else, even if she went to work as Tom Selleck's secretary, she thought with another despairing sob. She was in love with Elliott. Completely, incredibly, permanently in love. And it would take more than a new job for her to get him out of her heart, out of her mind. Much, much more.

HE HATED THE GUY. That David-What's-His-Name had pawed Mallory as if he'd had every right to do so, and what's worse, she'd let him! Encouraged him, even!

Slamming the door to his office, Elliott paced furiously from one end of the cluttered room to the other, fuming. How dare she allow some other man to hug her, kiss her cheek, when she'd made love with Elliott only hours before? And then to introduce the other man as "one of her best friends" while Elliott had been identified only as her "boss"—that had been the final straw, as far as he was concerned. Her boss. She could at least have called him another friend.

It briefly occurred to him that he'd been the one to pretty much ignore her all day, that he'd known she was hurt and confused by his distant behavior. But that was beside the point, he told himself resentfully. He still hadn't expected her to throw herself into the arms of another man the minute they arrived back in Dallas. A well-built, blond, lifeguard-type man. A man with what seemed to be a well-developed, genial sense of humor, an outgoing, friendly personality, a rakish sense of style that any woman would probably admire. A man with the self-confidence to show his feelings without wondering how he'd be interpreted, whether he was risking rebuff.

Growing more morose with each recollection of Mallory's friend's virtues, Elliott slumped into a chair and dejectedly pushed his hair off his forehead. Dammit, the guy was perfect for Mallory. Just her type. She deserved someone like that—someone normal. Someone who'd fit in with her friends. Someone who wouldn't make love to her one night, then retreat from her in near panic the next morning. Someone distinctly unlike Elliott.

He never should have allowed himself to fall in love. He wasn't the type who could handle it. If something didn't fit neatly into a well-defined, easily identifiable, practically applied subcategory, Elliott didn't quite know what to do about it. And neither Mallory nor his complex emotions toward her came close to being so easily pigeonholed.

It had been relatively easy to go along with the charade for a while, to play the role of confident, self-assured lover. But that had been acting. Once the emotions became reality, those old, nagging feelings of inadequacy had returned to plague him. What if he messed up? What if she changed her mind? What if he drove her away? What if she walked away on her own? So many questions, so much at stake. No practical formula for minimizing the possibilities of failure.

He thought of his colleagues at Option Forum. What would they do, he wondered wryly, if he presented this particular problem at their next session? Serious-natured, socially inept owl falls desperately in love with charming, self-confident hummingbird. What steps can he take to ensure that said hummingbird would never grow bored with him, never give in to a secret longing to return to her impetuous flower flitting, leaving poor owl alone in the darkness?

His colleagues would have him declared mentally incompetent. Ban him from their select ranks. Those among them with a sense of humor, no matter how slight, would laugh themselves silly.

Conclusion? The brilliant, nationally respected, frequently published and much-sought-after professor, scientist and inventor straightened in his chair, thrust a hand through his disordered auburn hair and curled his lip as he summed up his carefully thought-out hypothesis in two precise, loudly stated words.

"Love sucks."

MALLORY HAD BEEN at her desk for only a few minutes when Elliott made his appearance on Monday morning, his arms loaded with books and papers. He was obviously on his way out; Mallory assumed he would avoid her again by spending most of his time at the university. Stifling a sigh, she studied him, noting that he appeared to have slept no better than she had the night before. She supposed there was some small satisfaction in that, anyway.

He set a stack of neatly hand-written notes in front of her. "I'll need these typed by tomorrow morning." There was no emotion in his voice as he clipped out the instructions.

"I'll do them this afternoon," she promised, striving to sound equally distant.

He nodded. "Fine. I'll be at the university most of the day. Anything we need to discuss before I leave?"

She wondered what he meant by that. Was he referring to business or personal discussion? Either way, her answer was the same. "No. Nothing at all."

He nodded again and their eyes met. She thought she detected a fleeting look of pain in his dark gaze before he deliberately shuttered his expression. She wondered if she'd only imagined it. "Mallory—"

"Yes?"

He sighed and ran a hand through his neatly combed hair. "About the other night—"

She gulped, unprepared for him to bring up their lovemaking now. She'd fully expected him to continue to ignore the topic, as he so often seemed to do whenever anything became too personal, too uncomfortable for him. Taking a deep breath for courage, she asked rather too curtly, "What about it?"

"It meant a great deal to me," he replied with devastating simplicity. "I'm not sorry it happened. But I've been doing a great deal of thinking, and I've decided you were right. We allowed ourselves to be carried away by the roles we were playing. We're co-workers and, I hope, friends, and it would be best if we didn't jeopardize what we have by becoming involved in an affair."

"I agree." She dimly wondered how it was possible to speak so calmly and clearly while feeling as though someone had just slammed a fist into her midsection. "I've said all along that we were much too different to attempt anything more serious than friendship."

His jaw twitched, but he nodded quite coolly. "Yes, I know you have. One of the many lessons you tried to teach me, wasn't it? I simply didn't catch on to the trick of controlling my fantasies as easily as I learned driving and dancing."

Something in his voice—bitterness? self-disgust? regret?—made her squirm in her chair and unconsciously hold out a hand to him. "Elliott?"

He took a step backward, looking pointedly at his watch. "I'm glad we've gotten this behind us now so we can get on with our professional relationship. We have a lot to do in the next few weeks. I have to get ready for a new term at the university, and Option Forum's quarterly session is coming up soon."

"I'm certainly prepared to do whatever is necessary for my job," Mallory informed him. She looked forward to being busy, actually. She hoped she'd be so inundated with work so that at the office, at least, there'd be no time for self-pity, for futile thoughts of what might have been. At the office, at least, there'd be no time for tears.

Which didn't, of course, explain why she spent a good fifteen minutes sobbing into her typewriter after Elliott left for the university.

"HAND ME THAT WRENCH, will you, baby?"

Mallory lifted the requested tool and placed it into her father's broad, grease-stained hand. "This one?"

"Yep. Thanks. Stand back, now, you don't want to get your clothes dirty."

"Daddy, I wore old clothes so I could help you work on my car, not to stand back and watch you work."

Bill lifted his head from beneath the hood of the Ford long enough to give his daughter a quick, indulgent grin. "Well, it's a nice thought, but I've let you help before, remember, kid? Believe me, it's better this way. Safer for me *and* the car."

Mallory exhaled glumly and propped her elbows on the dented blue fender, her chin cradled in her hands. For the next ten minutes she watched her father manipulate the tangle of alien-looking parts of her car engine, the silence punctuated only by her occasional sigh. Finally Bill cleared his throat loudly and swiveled his head to frown at her. "You want to talk about it?"

She opened her eyes wide. "Talk about what?"

"Whatever it is that has you sounding like an old tire with a slow leak. Something's obviously bothering you."

She lifted a shoulder in a dispirited shrug. "Nothing major."

He went back to work, but didn't allow the subject to drop. "You've done it again, haven't you?"

"Done what again?"

"You've fallen for your boss. You'd think you'd have learned a lesson that last time."

"This isn't anything like last time!" Mallory protested, indignant at the very thought of comparing her feelings for Elliott with her silly infatuation with Larry.

"Yeah? What's different about it?"

"Larry was a shallow, self-centered jerk. Elliott is— Elliott is—" Appalled to find herself very close to bursting into tears, Mallory swallowed the words she was seeking.

Giving a final twist to whatever he'd been adjusting, Bill slammed the hood of Mallory's car and wiped his hands on a stained shop towel, his sharp gray eyes focused intently on his daughter's unhappy face. "This *is* different, isn't it?"

She nodded miserably.

"So what are you going to do about it?"

She shrugged. "I don't know. For a time, I thought— I hoped— But now he says we're too different and we shouldn't get involved, and I know he's probably right, but I wish— And every day for the past week, I've gone to work and it's so hard not to— And he seems unhappy, but he won't talk to me, and even when he smiles at something I say, he's holding back, and he didn't do that before— And, oh, Daddy, what am I going to do?"

Seeming to have followed her disjointed monologue without undue confusion, Bill twisted his mouth into a wryly sympathetic expression and slung an arm around Mallory's shoulders as he turned with her toward the house. "Let's go have some of your mother's cherry pie. She took one out of the oven just a while ago. We'll talk about it while we eat."

"So this guy thinks he's too smart for you," Bill commented fifteen minutes later after he'd pulled the entire story from Mallory—with the exclusion, of course, of their lovemaking after the party on Saturday night.

Mallory shook her head vehemently. "No, Daddy. Elliott has never treated me as anything less than an equal, though, of course, he is much more intelligent than I am."

Bill scowled. "Nonsense. You were third in your graduating high school class, top graduate in your secretarial college. Your teachers always said you could have applied yourself a little harder if you'd wanted to, but nobody ever said you weren't intelligent. Did you tell your genius boss that?"

Rolling her eyes, Mallory shook her head. "Daddy, being third in a graduating class of one hundred and fifty hardly compares to Elliott. He had his doctorate by age nineteen! He writes, invents, lectures, consults. He can do *anything* with a computer. It's not that he considers himself so much better than anyone else, but he really is very special."

"Elliott's a man," Bill argued stubbornly. "No better, no worse, than anyone else. And if he hasn't got sense to know he'd be lucky to have a bright, pretty, sweet-natured, kind-hearted girl like you, then I don't think he's all that smart, anyway."

Mallory smiled ruefully at her amused mother, who had been listening quietly to the exchange. Then she turned her eyes to her father. "Did it occur to you that you just might be a tad prejudiced?"

"I don't care. I won't have you thinking you're not good enough for this guy. I don't know what his problem is, but I know you can't spend the rest of your life moping around after him. So what are you going to do about it?"

This time Mallory gave the question several moments of consideration before answering. "You're right," she said finally. "I can't spend the rest of my life moping after Elliott. I've got more spunk than that."

"Damn right," Bill muttered approvingly.

Her spine straightening, chin lifting, Mallory tossed her ponytail defiantly. "And, darn it, I *am* good enough for Elliott Fraser! It's *his* hang-up standing between us."

"You bet it is."

"Right. So I'm going to stop moping and start enjoying myself again—with or without Elliott. If he wants to take a chance that we could have something special together, he knows where to find me."

"Good girl."

"Right."

"Right."

Moving with new determination, Mallory stood and soundly kissed her father's sun-leathered cheek. "Thanks, Daddy. For working on the car—and for the moral support."

"You're welcome, babe."

"Thanks for the pie, Mom. It was delicious, as always."

"Of course, darling." Jean hugged her warmly. "Give me a call if you want to talk later, all right?"

"Sure. I've got to go now. I have my Sunday afternoon laundry to do. Got to look fresh and professional when I show up at the office tomorrow."

Riding the wave of renewed energy her talk with her father had given her, Mallory swept out of the house, leaving her parents laughing in fond bewilderment at their daughter's mercurial moods.

ELLIOTT WASN'T QUITE SURE how to take Mallory's change of behavior during the next week. The week before she'd been quiet, rather subdued, doing her job with crisp, distant efficiency. Now it was as if the Mallory he'd known in the beginning had reappeared, as if the incident in Chicago had never even happened. She was friendly, chatty, good-humored. Greeting him each morning with a bright, cheerful smile, resuming her teasing about his cluttered office and his haphazard working habits. Several times he found himself responding to her without thought, drawn by the magnetic charm he'd admired in her from the first.

It was getting harder all the time to remember his logical, practical reasons for not allowing her to get too close, for not giving in to his all-too-frequent impulses to grab her and taste her endearingly crooked smile, to allow his hands to follow their urges to reacquaint themselves with her warm, responsive curves. He'd gone back to taking cold showers during the nights, and they were no more successful now than they'd been before he'd made love to her.

He couldn't help speculating about her abrupt change of attitude. What had caused it? Why was she treating him so casually, as if they'd never been more than friends? Had she come to the conclusion that she was glad they'd put a halt to their growing intimacy before they went too far with it?

He was still wondering about what was going on in that charming head of hers on Friday morning when he crossed the hall, planning to dictate a letter, and accidentally overheard her talking on the telephone. It was only when he heard the name David that *accidentally* turned to *purposefully*. Leaning against the wall just outside her opened office door, he grimly eavesdropped as she laughed at something the man said.

"David, you idiot," Mallory said in what Elliott could only describe as a crooning voice. She paused a moment, then laughed again. "All right, all right, I'd hate for you to wither up and die of loneliness. I'll go with you to the concert tonight—even though you know full well that I hate country and western music. I don't care if you *do* accuse me of being a traitor to Texas, I still like rock! Six-thirty? Sure, I can be ready by then. But I'm warning you, you're going to have to feed me well to make this worth my time. Mmm, sounds good. See you at six-thirty, David. 'Bye."

Elliott Fraser had never resorted to physical violence in his life. He'd always considered such behavior beneath the dignity of a truly civilized, inherently intelligent man. So, he told himself, taking several long, deep breaths, he wasn't really standing here considering strangling a tall, blond, lifeguard-type he'd met only briefly in an airport. Nor was he strongly tempted to drape one irresistible, attractive redhead over his knee and beat the living daylights out of her for daring to flirt with said lifeguard-type, to actually accept a date with him after making spectacular love to *him* only two weeks before!

No, he told himself again, whirling toward his office, the dictation forgotten. He wouldn't resort to violence. It simply wasn't in him to do so. Instead, he slammed his office door with enough force to rattle every one of the many windows in the two-story building.

Across the hall, Mallory jumped at the abrupt, teeth-jarring noise, her hand going to her pounding chest as she stared at her own open doorway. Why in the world was Elliott slamming doors? she wondered in bewilderment. And then her eyes focused on the telephone receiver she'd just replaced in its cradle.

Could he have overheard her conversation with David?

Would he have cared if he had?

Remembering the force of that door slamming, she bit her lip against a sudden, decidedly feline smile as she turned her attention back to the report she'd been typing before answering the telephone.

ELLIOTT'S FINGERS DRUMMED furiously on the leather-covered wheel of the Corvette as he sat parked in the shadows just down the street from Mallory's house. He checked the luminous dial of his watch for perhaps the two hundredth time in the past hour.

Midnight. Where the hell was she?

Even as he asked himself the question, he wasn't so sure he wanted to know the answer. It was all too easy to picture her with the other man, laughing, chattering—he swallowed painfully—making love. Dammit.

He shifted restlessly in the deep leather seat as his body reacted to memories of Mallory in bed with him that night after his grandparents' party. He could still see her so clearly, her green eyes luminous in the dim light, her hair tumbling wantonly around her bare, gold-dusted shoulders, her face taut with desire and then soft with satisfaction. The echo of her quiet, throaty cries of pleasure seemed to fill the hauntingly silent interior of the Corvette, followed by his deep groan.

He checked his watch again. Twelve-fifteen. Maybe she wasn't coming home. Maybe she was spending the night with that—

He stiffened as a set of headlights came down the street, then turned into Mallory's driveway before passing the Corvette. Thank God. She was home.

But what if the other guy stayed?

His jaw squaring, Elliott decided to give the jerk ten minutes to clear out. And then he would—

What? Muttering a curse, he shoved a hand through already wildly disordered hair and asked himself just what he intended to do if Mallory invited the other man to her bed for the night. It wasn't as if Elliott had any sort of claim over her. After all, he'd made it quite clear he didn't intend to pick up where they'd left off in Chicago. He couldn't blame Mallory for choosing to go on with her social life, nor expect her to spend her Friday evenings alone.

But it hurt, he discovered, slowly rubbing his chest as if the pain were, indeed, real. It hurt badly.

He almost slumped in relief when Mallory's date did not accompany her inside her house, spending only a moment on her doorstep before dropping a light, friendly looking kiss on her lips and leaving with a cheery wave. Elliott's eyes closed tightly. By the time he reopened them, the other man was gone, and Mallory was safely inside her house. Alone.

Elliott leaned back in the seat, his thoughts grim with self-disgust. He wondered bleakly if he'd regressed to the foolish adolescence he'd never really had as a youth. He was certainly acting like a lovesick schoolboy, jealously spying on his popular girlfriend. He didn't like himself very much tonight.

He'd been a fool, he realized abruptly, his hand clenching into a fist. A fool to give up so easily after finding something most men would gladly die for. What had happened between Mallory and him hadn't been a fluke. He hadn't been carried away with a charade, acting out feelings that hadn't been real. What they'd shared had been vitally serious, explosive, incredible. It had existed before their charade had begun—from the moment, in fact, when their eyes had met in the reception area of that employment agency. What they'd shared had overpowered their best efforts to avoid it and, dammit, it hadn't gone away just because Elliott had decided he wasn't quite brave enough to deal with it.

Mallory thought they were too different to become involved, but she hadn't been able to hide her unhappiness from him since they'd returned from Chicago. Despite her more cheerful behavior of the past week, he knew he wasn't wrong in believing that she was no more immune to him now than he was to her. So what he had to do, he decided with clear, concise logic, was to convince her that they weren't so different, after all. He had to start all over, salvaging the friendship they'd formed in those first lighthearted weeks. Then he would try to convince her that they could have much, much more than friendship.

He'd give her the rest of the weekend—give himself the rest of the weekend to prepare—and then he'd begin his campaign on Monday. He was in love with her, and he wasn't going to give up on that love without making one hell of an effort to convince her that he could make her happy.

10

"GOOD MORNING, MALLORY."

At the unexpectedly cheery greeting, Mallory looked up in surprise from the desk drawer where she'd just stashed her purse in preparation for her working day. "Um—good morning, Elliott."

He sauntered toward her desk, smiling broadly. "Have a nice weekend?"

"Why, yes, thank you. And you?" she asked politely, though her mind was spinning. The last time she'd seen him had been Friday afternoon, and he'd been in a royal sulk—she'd assumed because of the telephone conversation she suspected he'd overheard. Now he was smiling more naturally than he had in weeks. What was going on?

"Very nice. Those papers stacked on your desk are some notes I need typed up in preparation for the Option Forum session next week."

"I'll get right on them."

"By the way, I was looking at your calendar earlier to see what was on my agenda for the next week, and I noticed the notation for this Friday night. 'Party—7:00 p.m.' Is that one of my functions or yours?"

Still a little suspicious of his blandly friendly behavior, she glanced at the calendar and then back up at him. "Mine. It's just another get-together my friends are planning."

"Mmm. Are you going with a date?" he asked, leaning a hip against the edge of her desk and watching her with not-very-well-concealed intentness.

She lifted a brow at the personal question, but was surprised into answering honestly. "Well, no, I hadn't planned on going with anyone."

His smile was quick and almost blindingly bright. "Will you allow me to take you?"

She swallowed, staring at him, wondering if maybe she was still sleeping and only dreaming that it was Monday morning and she was in her office talking to a strange man in Elliott's body. "You?" she managed weakly.

"Mmm," he said again, nodding. "You know. A date?"

"But, Elliott—"

He rose abruptly from the desk, turning toward the doorway. "Good. I'll look forward to it. Guess I'd better get busy now. There's a ton of work to be done before next week."

Realizing she was staring after him with a gaping mouth, Mallory snapped her jaws shut and shook her head as if to clear it. And then she pinched her arm. Hard.

"I'm awake," she muttered, staring at the reddening spot beneath her fingers. "Maybe Elliott's the one who's sleepwalking."

Had he really just asked her for a date on Friday night? To another party with her friends, for heaven's sake? Surely not. He hated parties. He wasn't too crazy about her friends. And he had flatly told her that he only wanted a professional relationship with her from now on. Surely she'd misunderstood.

"Oh, and Mallory?"

Her head swiveled toward the man leaning into her doorway. "Yes, Elliott?"

"Is this another casual evening? I'd like to be dressed correctly this time."

"Yes, it'll be very casual. But, Elliott—"

"That's all I needed to know. Let me know if you have any questions about those notes, okay? I'll be in the pit." He flashed her a grin and disappeared.

For the second time Mallory closed her mouth and then stood and headed for the small storage room off her office where she kept a coffee maker. "Coffee," she murmured dazedly. "I need coffee. Very strong coffee."

Across the hallway, Elliott's grin lingered as he bent over his computer. He'd enjoyed that, he decided with an unfamiliar rush of mischief. Mallory had spent the past week confusing him with her changing moods and behavior; she deserved to have a little of her own medicine spooned down her throat.

It might just be an interesting—and rather amusing—week.

"ELLIOTT, you're going to have to hurry or you'll be late for your class," Mallory reminded her employer two mornings later, finding him still engrossed in a new computer program he was designing. She held his briefcase in her hands, prepared to shove it at him and push him out the door, knowing how hard it was to get his attention when he was involved so deeply in one of his projects.

He glanced up impatiently from the computer screen, then turned right back to it, muttering, "Yeah, okay, just a minute."

She moved across his office with determined strides, stopping inches away from him. "Elliott, you haven't got a minute. You have to leave now. You can work on that when you get back this afternoon."

"Mallory, I—" Impatience still laced his voice as he turned toward her again. This time his words died as his gaze collided with the low front of her gold sweater. He obviously hadn't noticed that she'd moved closer.

When she realized how long his eyes lingered on the hint of cleavage revealed by her scoop-necked top, Mallory shifted uncomfortably and loudly cleared her throat. "Elliott, you have to go. Now," she added flatly, shoving the briefcase at him and hoping he wasn't aware of the wave of color starting somewhere around the base of her neck and inching upward. For the past two days he'd been doing this to her—looking at her in a way that somehow reminded her of that magic moment when he'd first spotted her standing in the doorway of their connecting bathroom in his grandparents' house. Each time he looked at her that way, her body went into reckless overdrive.

Fully distracted now from the computer, Elliott nodded slowly and stored what he'd done. "Okay, I'm going." He straightened and took the briefcase from her, then almost knocked the breath out of her by running one fingertip very lightly across the swath of skin exposed at her neckline. "Nice sweater," he commented, his voice slightly husky. And then he left, telling her brusquely that he'd be back immediately after conducting his class at the university.

Mallory managed a semi-coherent reply, but it was a full five minutes before she could convince her legs to do their intended job and carry her steadily into her own office.

Ten minutes later she almost had herself convinced that she hadn't been deliberately dressing in the most flattering, attractive outfits she owned that were still suitable for the office. And then she found herself wondering what she'd wear the next day, her thoughts lingering on a lacy blouse that would knock her employer's mismatched socks off.

Realizing what she was doing, she buried her face in her hands and groaned, convinced she'd finally lost her mind completely.

"BY THE WAY," Elliott interrupted his dictation to ask as the thought suddenly occurred to him sometime Thursday morning, "have you made our reservations yet?"

Confused by the sudden shift in topics, Mallory looked up from her notebook to the chair beside her desk where Elliott lounged comfortably. "Reservations?"

"Mmm. For California. We'll need two round-trip tickets and then, of course, a suite at the hotel. The name and phone number of the hotel are in the Option Forum file."

"Elliott, does this mean you expect me to go with you to California?" Mallory asked blankly. This was the first reference he'd made to both of them going; she'd just assumed he'd be out of town for a week or so and expect her to handle the office while he was gone.

Elliott frowned at her question. "Well, of course, I expect you to go. You're my secretary. Everyone brings a secretary along—well, almost everyone. Sybil always accompanied me."

"But what would I do?"

"Plenty. Take notes during the brainstorming sessions, type them up each evening before the next morning's meeting, be available for dictation whenever I need to prepare a report to submit to the group, handle the calls and correspondence I'll receive as a member of the Forum, take care of—"

"Okay, I get the picture," Mallory interrupted. She twisted her pencil between suddenly unsteady fingers. A week or more in California with Elliott, she thought, torn between anticipation and dread at the idea.

Would they be able to spend that time together without giving in to desire again? Would they find themselves falling into bed, reliving the passion they'd discovered in Chicago? And, if they did make love again, would Elliott then retreat within himself upon the return home, as he had the last time? She honestly thought it would destroy her if he did that to her again.

And yet, what could she do? She *was* his secretary. It was her job to accompany him on such business trips. She could either quit and allow him to find someone with the courage to fulfill her duties, or go with him.

She knew even as the choices occurred to her that she wouldn't—couldn't—quit.

So it seemed she'd be going to California with him. All she could do would be to try her best to stay out of his bed—and keep him out of hers—while they were there.

And then it occurred to her that she wouldn't necessarily have to lock her doors against him. It might be that he wouldn't even make the effort to seduce her.

She'd forgotten about Petra. Attractive, brilliant, once-willing Petra who, if the woman had any sense at all, would jump at the chance to be with Elliott again, Mallory thought glumly. She couldn't imagine any woman deliberately turning him away after having once been intimately involved with him.

Her chin firmed. She was definitely going with him to California. And she was going to do everything she could to keep him safely out of reach of his former lover, who'd been all wrong for him. Petra could never make him happy. Mallory couldn't stand by and watch him make himself miserable with a woman who didn't have the sensitivity and insight to know that there was so much more to love about Elliott than his IQ.

And if she failed, if he and Petra *did* resume their affair while they were in California next week, then Mallory would quietly, sensibly, very deliberately throw herself off the nearest cliff.

"Mallory?" Elliott was watching her oddly as he said her name to reclaim her attention. "Is there a problem?"

She wondered uncomfortably what emotions might have crossed her face in the past few moments. "No, Elliott," she assured him coolly. "No problem at all. You said we needed a suite?"

"Yes. Two bedrooms and a sitting room. We'll use the sitting room for a temporary office. The hotel staff is familiar with my usual requests."

"Fine." She held her pencil poised over her notepad. "Are you ready to finish this letter now?"

Elliott was still watching her closely, but at her brusque question he nodded and lowered his eyes. "Read back what I've said so far," he ordered.

MALLORY TRIED to keep her hands steady as she tied the enormous black bow that secured the bottom of her French braid. It wasn't easy since she knew that any moment her doorbell would ring, announcing Elliott's arrival to pick her up for the party. She still didn't know why he'd asked to take her, still wasn't certain what lay behind his congenial behavior during the past few days, had no more clue to what he really wanted from her than she had the day they'd returned from Chicago. And yet she could no more have turned down a chance to spend an evening with him than she could have changed herself with a wave of her hand from a terminally cute, green-eyed redhead to a sultry, olive-skinned brunette.

Stepping back from her dressing table, she checked her appearance one last time. Made of soft cotton knit, her two-piece outfit consisted of a swingy, black and white waist-length top over a matching gored miniskirt. Her jewelry was chunky, black and white plastic, her shoes black flats. Not exactly glamorous, but not bad, she decided. Sybil, of course, wouldn't be caught dead in it. Nor, most likely, would Petra.

No, she thought defiantly, she wouldn't think that way. She was just Mallory, and she had no intention of trying to be anyone else—not even as an attempt to impress Elliott.

And then the doorbell rang. Mallory gulped, stared at the mirror for one last, long moment, and wished she'd worn something just a bit more sophisticated.

Wiping her damp palms on her skirt, she pulled open her front door only to do a classic double take at the man standing there smiling at her. Wearing pleated, whitewashed gray jeans with a gray and heather-plum geometric print sweater, sleeves pushed up on his muscular forearms, his dark red hair attractively mussed by the early-evening breeze, Elliott looked young and casual and stylish. He hardly resembled the rather stern, reserved professor who'd accompanied her to the last party with her friends. Even as she opened her mouth to greet him, she found herself fighting the almost overwhelming urge to throw herself on his gorgeous body.

"Elliott, you look—great," she said, for lack of a more appropriately complimentary word.

He almost beamed with his pleasure. "Thanks. Like the clothes? I bought them this afternoon."

"*You* went shopping? Alone?"

"Yeah," he said proudly. "But I have to confess I had a lot of help from a friendly salesclerk." And then his grin widened as he tugged upward on one leg of his jeans. "Check this out."

She couldn't help but laugh at his pride in the gray and plum argyle socks that matched his sweater almost perfectly. "It's a very nice ensemble," she assured him.

"Ensemble, huh?" He nodded as he said the word. "Yeah, that's what the clerk called it. So, you think I'll fit in with your friends this time?"

The question caught her off guard. More specifically, the trace of uncertainty behind the question made her pause before answering. She'd just told herself that she couldn't change to please Elliott; now she wondered if he were trying to change to impress her. It was a flattering thought, but just as futile. No relationship between two people could last long if one or both tried to fit into a role that simply wasn't real.

"Elliott, you really do look wonderful, but it wasn't necessary for you to go to so much trouble just to fit in with my friends. Believe me, you always look good to me," she told him with gentle candor.

His eyes softened visibly as he reached up to touch her cheek with one caressing finger. "Thanks, Mallory. That was a very nice thing to say. But I wanted to buy something new. I had a good time shopping for the first time in years, and I like the clothes. Inside, I'm still the same old Elliott Fraser, socially inept genius. Okay?"

She wrinkled her nose at him. "Socially inept, my behind," she retorted. "I'm beginning to think that was just a ploy to gain my sympathy. A very original line."

He chuckled and held the door open for her to pass him as she snatched up her black leather hobo bag. "So I've been caught out, have I?" he teased, slinging a casual arm around her as they headed for his car.

The bittersweet pleasure in their renewed camaraderie settled into a lump somewhere in her chest, but she made a special effort to keep her tone light as she returned his teasing. "You fraud. How many women have you talked into giving you dancing and driving lessons just so you'd have an excuse to make passes at them?"

"Oh, dozens," he assured her. "By the way," he added as he opened the passenger door of the Corvette, "you look good tonight. Almost as good as I do."

She was laughing when he firmly closed her inside.

Elliott's answering grin was one of sheer self-congratulation.

If Mallory had been surprised by Elliott's appearance and behavior that evening, those of her friends

who'd met him at the last party were even more startled. "Are you sure that's the same guy you were with
last time?" one woman asked in a dramatic stage whisper while Elliott attracted a laugh with a self-mocking
joke about absent-minded professors.

"No, I'm not sure about anything anymore," Mallory answered slowly, her eyes narrowing as she
watched the man-crazy Cindy inching her way closer
to Elliott's side. "Excuse me, Anne."

She pushed her way firmly through the crowd until
she was close to Elliott, noting in displeasure that Cindy
had reached him ahead of her. "It's good to see you
again, Professor," Cindy purred in her best smoke-and-
satin voice, her long-nailed fingers curling around his
arm. "Remember me?"

"Oh, yes," Elliott replied evenly, looking down at the
shapely brunette with a smile. "How are you, Cindy?"

Mallory gritted her teeth. Of *course* he remembered
Cindy, she fumed. No man ever forgot Cindy.

"I'm feeling lucky tonight," Cindy replied to Elliott's
polite question, her dark eyes glittering with mischief
and invitation. "Remember you told me you might give
me a demonstration of your kisses sometime if I was
lucky?"

Again, those who remembered the joke from the last
party snickered, several eyeing Mallory to see how she
was reacting to Cindy's blatant flirting with Mallory's
date. Mallory tried not to let it show that she was seriously considering pulling the other woman's eyelashes off—one by one.

Elliott's eyebrow rose speculatively. "You want a
demonstration of the way I kiss?" he asked, making

Mallory wonder seethingly just where he'd learned to inject such sexually teasing banter into his deep voice.

Cindy's gaze shot quickly toward Mallory, then back up to Elliott. Mallory wasn't at all surprised when Cindy's tone was bedroom smooth. "I would adore a demonstration, Professor."

Mallory decided right then that she was going to forget pulling eyelashes and go straight for Cindy's over-glossed lips. If Elliott actually touched his mouth to Cindy's, Mallory would—would—well, she'd do something violent, she decided.

And then she heard Elliott say laughingly, "All right, Cindy. You've got yourself a deal."

No one—least of all Mallory—expected his next move.

Before Mallory had a chance to react, she found herself draped backward over Elliott's arm, her mouth thoroughly possessed by his. The roar of appreciative laughter around them blended with the odd humming noise she recognized as a familiar accompaniment to Elliott's kisses until her head seemed filled with sound. Her body reacted immediately and dramatically to the embrace. The kiss probably lasted less than a minute, but it seemed like forever before Elliott raised his head, grinning wickedly down at Mallory for a moment before lifting her upright, and turned to Cindy. "Learn anything?"

Pouting good-naturedly, Cindy sighed. "That wasn't exactly what I had in mind by way of a demonstration."

"Sorry, that's the best I can do." Elliott turned back to Mallory who stood in stunned immobility by his side. "Dance with me?"

Dance? She could do that. Couldn't she? All she had to do first was remember how to walk. She cleared her throat. "Um—sure."

"Loosen up," Elliott urged her a few minutes later as they moved slowly across the dance floor to a sultry, slow number. "You're too tense." His teasing was a deliberate reminder of the many times she'd said the same thing to him during their dance lessons.

Mallory sighed and tilted her head back to stare up at him. "Elliott, what are you doing?"

He lifted a brow in inquiry. "Other than dancing with you?"

"Yes."

"I'm having a good time."

She frowned. "Are you really? Or are you just—"

"I'm really having a good time. Remember what I said the night of my grandparents' party? You've taught me how to enjoy myself."

She remembered many things from that night—all too well. "I don't know what's going on anymore," she said at last, admitting her confusion. "You're distant and formal one week and friendly and flirty the next. I never know what to expect from you."

"I could say the same about you."

She bit her lower lip, knowing he was right. "I—uh—"

The music ended. Elliott drew back, his gaze still locked with hers. "I don't think this is really the proper place to discuss it, do you?"

She shook her head. "No."

"We'll talk later," he promised. A new song began, this one the same pounding rock and roll number she'd selected during their last dancing lesson at his house.

He grinned. "They're playing our song, sweetheart." He held out his hand.

Unable to resist him when he smiled at her in just that way, she placed her hand in his. "Then let's not waste it."

BRINGING THE CORVETTE to a stop in Mallory's driveway, Elliott turned off the motor, then sat for a moment drumming his fingers on the wheel before turning to her. "I had a good time tonight."

"So did I," she admitted.

"You were right, you know."

"I was? About what?"

"Social small talk's not that hard. All you have to do is talk without really saying anything."

Startled into a giggle, Mallory nodded. "Basically, that's all it is."

He tilted his head thoughtfully. "But don't you and your friends ever talk about more serious subjects? Politics, current affairs, that sort of thing?"

"Of course we do, Elliott. Usually in smaller gatherings than tonight—say, when six or eight of us get together for dinner or a quiet evening at someone's house. You'd probably enjoy one of those evenings, though you'd have to keep in mind that not everyone is as well informed as you are."

Remembering the way he'd always seemed interested in her opinions about such subjects, no matter how shaky her background, she didn't for a moment believe that Elliott would have trouble talking with her friends. As a matter of fact, she thought fleetingly, some of the friends in her closest circle held rather impressive positions themselves, not that she would expect

Elliott to be any more impressed by their titles than Mallory was. Like Mallory, Elliott seemed more interested in personality than position, which was one of the many, many things she liked about him. Maybe, she thought wistfully, they had more in common than she'd allowed herself to hope. If only...

"Mallory, we can't go on like this."

She swiveled her head to stare at him in response to the gravely spoken words. Her mouth went dry. Was this his way of firing her? Of telling her he didn't want to see her again? That he no longer needed her for anything? "What—what do you mean?"

"I mean," he replied with obviously strained patience, "exactly what I said. We can't go on this way. We've been tiptoeing around each other for the past three weeks, trying to ignore what happened in Chicago, telling ourselves that it shouldn't have happened, that it mustn't happen again. And if I know you as well as I think I do, all our logical little speeches and decisions are working no better for you than they are for me. Am I wrong, or have you been as miserable as I have during these past two weeks?"

Maybe she could have lied to him if it hadn't been for the faintest trace of vulnerability she'd heard behind his question. Maybe she could have told him that she'd been just fine, that their night together hadn't haunted her at all. And maybe she could have made him believe her. "I don't think you could possibly have been as miserable as I have," she said instead.

"Mallory." He turned to her then, taking her shoulders in his hands as he strained to see her clearly in the diffused artificial lighting filtering into the car. "I have never wanted any other woman as much as I want you.

I've never felt for any other woman what I feel for you. I've spent so many nights lying awake, wanting you so badly I ached all over, remembering how it felt to have you next to me, beneath me, around me."

Mallory moaned, her body throbbing with the memories his words invoked, the needs those memories fueled.

"You say we're too different to make it together, that you're afraid to try for fear of getting hurt again," he went on inexorably. "I understand your fears because I feel them myself. I don't know what it would do to me if we were together for a time only to have you decide that I can't make you happy after all. Or even worse, for you to leave me for someone else. It almost drove me insane when you went out with that other guy last weekend. I wasn't going to tell you," he added rather sheepishly, "but I spent over an hour parked just down the street, waiting for you to get home, ready to smash that guy's face in if he dared try to stay with you."

Mallory felt her eyes widen in startled reaction to his confession, her heart pounding with hope—and panic. "You did that?"

"Yes. I'm not proud of it, but dammit, Mallory, I can't help myself! Sometimes I don't even know myself anymore. You do things to me. Things I don't understand. Things I don't quite know how to handle. And yet—"

"And yet?" she whispered when he hesitated, needing so desperately to hear what he had to say.

His fingers moved convulsively against her shoulders, his voice deepened when he continued. "And yet I can't help wondering if I was ever truly alive before you came into my life. I never understood just how

empty my life was until you came along and filled it
with fun and laughter and surprises. And this."

This was his mouth on hers, his arms hard around
her. *This* was need and hunger and desire so hot it siz-
zled in the close confines around them. *This* was his
breath, warm and ragged on her face as he muttered her
name between long, deep, drugging kisses. *This* was his
hand on her breasts beneath her loose-fitting top, his
fingers eagerly searching out the hard, puckered tips
that ached hungrily for his touch. His thigh hard
against hers, his back damp and vibrant beneath her
palms as they slid inside his sweater to flatten against
him.

Lost in a swirling gray world of sensual intoxica-
tion, oblivious to their surroundings, Mallory tried to
get closer, her hands voracious as they swept the body
that was so delightfully familiar to her, so desperately
beloved. She felt the moan that vibrated through him
as her hand fell to his thigh, then slowly, daringly
moved upward, finding him hard and throbbing and
so unmistakably hungry for her. Lovingly she stroked
him.

The tender caress seemed to send him over some invisible edge. Her name rumbling from his lips, he
pressed her back into her seat—only to suddenly pull
back with an exclamation of pain.

Blinking at the abrupt descent to reality, Mallory
reached out to him. "Elliott, what is it?"

His smile was visibly forced. "I came close to being
unmanned by the gear shift," he answered, his voice still
husky. "I think I've discovered the major disadvantage
in owning a sports car. It's damned hard to make love
in one—especially for someone over six feet."

She moistened her lips, her eyes meeting his. "We can always go inside. There's plenty of room in my bed."

He caught his breath, then released it in a slow, expressive gust. "No."

Her own breath stopped somewhere in her throat. "No?" she echoed in disbelief. He actually intended to stop now? Now, when she was still trembling all over, wanting him so badly she thought she'd shatter into frustrated bits if she couldn't have him?

"No," he repeated, more firmly this time. "Not as long as you still have doubts about us. You do, don't you?"

"Elliott, I—"

"Mallory, I want you. You know—surely you know—how much I want you. But I have to know that it's more than physical, for both of us. That what we feel—what we *both* feel—is real and lasting and stronger than any doubts you may have about whether we have enough in common, whether we can be happy together. I don't know what it will take to convince you that none of those differences matter, that we have so much more in common than you'll allow yourself to believe, but—"

"California."

Startled by the unexpected interruption, Elliott stopped and frowned at her. "What?"

"California," she repeated clearly, her hands twisting restlessly in her lap.

"I don't understand."

She took a deep breath. "You've shown me that you can get along just fine in my world, something I never doubted for a minute, anyway. You even seemed to enjoy yourself tonight, which rather surprised me, I'll admit. Now we have to see how well I fit into your world."

"What about the faculty reception you attended with me? You handled that beautifully. You work with me every day, and you've done an excellent job of that. And you charmed the socks off my family in Chicago. How can you say that you don't know how well you fit into my world?"

She didn't know how to explain her qualms about California. That she felt much more threatened by the exclusively brilliant think tank than she had by anything else between them. That she was convinced that if anything would make him realize how very different they were, it would be this time he would spend with his peers in Option Forum. She certainly had no intention of mentioning Petra just now. Now knowing what to say, she said nothing.

He gave her another moment, then finally sighed and released her. "All right. We'll wait until we get back from California to continue this. Not that I think anything will change."

"I think that would be best," she managed, though she wanted nothing more than to drag him forcibly into her apartment and chain him to her bed.

"All right, then. Just promise me one thing, will you?"

"What?" she asked warily.

"Don't keep shutting me out. It hurts when you do that."

She reached out to touch her fingers lightly to his cheek. "All right."

He smiled at her, though the smile didn't quite reach his eyes. "I'll walk you to the door."

"Fine."

He kissed her at her door, lightly, holding himself in rigid restraint. He had just turned to walk back to his car when she spoke impulsively. "Elliott—if it makes any difference, I was miserable on my date with David, even though he's just a friend. I kept thinking of you, wishing I were with you."

He groaned and pulled her to him for a quick, hard kiss. "You know how to stretch my willpower to the limits, don't you?" he asked, trying for a light, teasing tone and failing. "But thank you, Mallory. It does make a difference. Good night."

"Good night." She closed the door behind her quickly, before either of them could say anything more.

11

THE DOOR TO THE UNIVERSITY conference room loomed in front of her like the main gate to the underworld. Mallory stood still, her sensibly heeled business pumps seemingly glued to the tastefully plush carpeting beneath them, her steno book clasped tightly to the chest of the taupe linen jacket of her plain, executive-secretary-type suit.

Coming to a halt beside her, Elliott frowned curiously, questioning her sudden immobility. "Mallory? This is the meeting room. Let's go in."

"I'm not sure I can," she whispered through stiff lips, still staring at that ominously heavy door.

Chuckling, Elliott slipped an arm around her waist. "Come on. What do you expect to find waiting in there?" he chided.

Fighting a mental image of evil demons wearing academic caps and gowns, she managed a shrug of sorts. "Geniuses."

He laughed at that, his arm tightening in a comforting hug. "Geniuses and their secretaries," he corrected her teasingly.

She rolled her eyes at him. "That doesn't help."

"Mallory, they're my friends. They're very nice people. And, like everyone else you meet, they'll be eating out of your enchanting little hands before an hour has passed. Now take a deep breath, keep up your chin and let's get to work, shall we?"

"But, Elliott, I can't take notes in Latin," she blurted inanely.

His dark eyes dancing, he nodded gravely, managing not to smile. "That's perfectly all right. We usually conduct our sessions in English. However, if I forget and lapse into one of the classical languages, just give me a nudge."

She frowned at him. "You're laughing at me."

He dropped a fleeting, whisper-soft kiss on the end of her nose. "I'm enjoying you, Mallory. I'm very glad you're here."

Melting at his words—as he'd probably known she would, the rat—Mallory allowed herself to be led through the doors behind which Elliott's fellow think tank members waited.

She'd seen them all before in the photograph in Elliott's office. Her initial amusement returned full force when she actually met them in person. As Elliott introduced her to each of his associates who, in turn, introduced their own assistants, Mallory noted that the Option Forum members were civil enough in their greetings but notably different from most people she knew. Identified as professors, scientists, economists, and/or sociologists, each bore an aura of self-absorption, wearing expressions that seemed to indicate their thoughts were turned toward higher pursuits, leaving little time for the polite conventions of society. She'd seen Elliott look just that way at times, she thought with a sudden flash of recognition. Funny how it was so much more endearing from Elliott.

Polyester slacks worn too short, outdated ties, plastic pocket protectors holding pencils and markers, horn-rimmed glasses held together with white tape. As she shook hands and memorized names, she noted each stereotypical feature with an almost fond indulgence that went a long way toward soothing her over-strained nerves.

And then Elliott's fingers tightened where they'd lain loosely at the small of her back, and she heard him say, "Mallory Littlefield, I'd like you to meet Dr. Petra Jantzen."

Mallory had studied Petra's photograph more than once during the past week in making herself ready to meet her face to face. She'd been prepared to meet an attractive brunette with a permanently serious expression and a strict, no-nonsense wardrobe. She hadn't realized that Petra was, quite simply, beautiful.

The severely knotted styling of her coal-black hair served only to emphasize Petra's classically perfect bone structure. Though a touch of makeup would have highlighted her best features, its absence emphasized the creamy flawlessness of her complexion. Rather than hiding her well-spaced, brightly intelligent violet eyes, her oversized glasses framed them beautifully. And her simply tailored, plainly styled teal-blue dress could only have looked that good on someone with a tall, slender, well-conditioned figure—a figure exactly like Petra's.

Mallory's ego dropped straight down to the bottom of her shoes.

"It's very nice to meet you," Petra murmured in a clear, beautifully modulated voice. Her eyes lingered for a moment on Elliott's hand, resting now at Mallory's waist, before lifting to his face. "Sybil isn't with you this time?"

"No. Sybil doesn't work for me now. She's getting married in a couple of weeks and moving to Hawaii." Though she listened intently, Mallory could detect nothing more in Elliott's reply than the same friendly warmth he'd displayed toward the others in the room.

"You must be sure to give her my congratulations," Petra instructed Elliott with a slight smile.

"I'll do that. Thank you."

"We have quite a full agenda today, so perhaps we'd better get started," said a thin, balding professor Elliott had identified as Dr. Marcus Rosenzweig, chairman of Option Forum. Obediently the twelve think tank members and the eight secretarial assistants accompanying them settled at a conference table that would have comfortably accommodated ten more people.

Valiantly attempting to take notes on proceedings that occasionally left her thoroughly bewildered, Mallory spent the next few hours closely observing Elliott's associates and watching Elliott as he interacted with them. It was obvious from the start that he was completely at home with the group, that he enjoyed their work, thriving on the challenges presented to him. Her heart sank at the thought that she could never offer that kind of intellectual stimulation. Didn't that matter at all to him? she wondered bleakly.

The group's primary purpose seemed to be to offer viable solutions to problems presented to them from a variety of corporate and educational institutions from around the country. The discussions were lively, sometimes heated, always serious. Several times one of the assistants was dispatched to the university library to obtain research materials to aid in the brainstorming. Lunch consisted of sandwiches eaten between sentences.

No clowning, Mallory noted as she surreptitiously massaged her neck sometime during the afternoon. The occasional light remark was always greeted with a polite round of smiles that faded almost immediately back into the sober, furrowed expressions of deep thought. Elliott was as bad as the rest of them, she thought glumly. Where was the witty humor she'd seen in him so many times, the ready laughter?

"Dull bunch, aren't they?" a rather chubby, fortyish ash blonde murmured to Mallory as they broke for mid-afternoon coffee. Elliott was standing with his colleagues in one corner of the huge room, involved in a discussion that was no more than a continuation of the conference. So much for a break, Mallory thought, turning her eyes to the other secretary who had spoken to her in the corner where the assistants had gathered to stretch and sip their coffee or soft drinks.

"I wondered if I was the only one who noticed," she said in response to the other woman's observation. "I don't suppose they get 'the simples' when they get tired later on?" she asked hopefully.

The older woman chuckled and shook her head. "Honey, they don't *get* tired. And not a one of them would do anything so frivolous as to indulge in a case of 'the simples' in front of the others. My name's Joan, by the way. You're Mallory, aren't you?"

"Yes. You work for Dr. Michaelson?"

"Have for the past eleven years," Joan confirmed cheerfully. "One thing I can say for the job, it rarely gets dull. Coping with the volatile temperament of genius, you know. And he pays well. How long have you been with Dr. Fraser? I understand his sister quit to get married."

"Yes. I haven't been with him very long." *Only long enough to change my entire life.*

"He seems like a nice man."

"Yes. He is."

Seeming to read something in Mallory's voice—or perhaps her expression—Joan looked thoughtfully at the younger woman. "They're not easy men to be involved with, you know. It's sometimes hard playing second fiddle to a computer or a logic problem."

Mallory's eyes widened in surprise at the other woman's perception. "I—uh—"

"Oh, honey, I know the signs," Joan assured her airily. "You're nuts about the guy."

"Well, I—"

"You don't really think I'd have stayed with Walter all these years for the money, do you?"

Mallory looked from Joan to the short, greying economist now talking to Elliott. "You mean you and Dr. Michaelson—?"

"Have been living together for ten and a half years," Joan confirmed with a smile. "Walter proposed three or four years ago, but he hasn't gotten around to doing anything about it yet. I'm waiting for him to remember that we still haven't actually done it, but I may be forced to just set a date and drive him to a justice of the peace eventually."

Mallory bit her lip to keep from laughing, but failed to stop the gurgle of amusement from escaping. "I'm sorry."

Laughing with her, Joan shook her head. "Don't apologize. I accepted long ago—when I first fell in love with the guy—that I was giving up any chance of a 'normal' life by tying myself to him. I've never regretted it, however. Those few occasions when I have his full attention—well, they make it all worth it."

"But doesn't it bother you," Mallory asked carefully, "that he's so—so brilliant, so awesomely intellectual?"

"It did at first," Joan agreed. "I was afraid he'd become bored with me, lose interest in my opinions. But then I realized that he needed me, needed someone who wasn't always challenging him or expecting something from him, needed someone to just let him be himself and relax. They're geniuses, true, but they're also human, you know."

Which was exactly what Mallory had said from the beginning, she realized with a start. When had she stopped criticizing his family for treating him as no more than a brain and begun to do so herself? she wondered. Why had she let her own insecurities about their relationship blind her to the needs she'd sensed in Elliott from the beginning?

She spent the rest of the afternoon watching him again, this time as a man who enjoyed his work, a special, talented, but so-very-human man. The man she loved. And she told herself that she had so much to offer him, if he wanted it. Which he seemed to do. But how was she to tell him she wanted another chance with him? Should she bring it up, or should she wait until he said something about their relationship?

Chewing on her lower lip, she tried to concentrate on her work, not an easy task since her thoughts were so fully absorbed with Elliott.

AT SIX O'CLOCK the group adjourned for the day. All but two of them were staying at the same hotel where Mallory and Elliott were lodged, due to its proximity to the Berkeley campus where Option Forum always convened. Some of the others mentioned meeting in the hotel restaurant for dinner, but Elliott did not commit himself and Mallory to join them, she noticed. He was more abstracted than usual, still absorbed in a problem that had been tabled until the next day, since no immediate solution had presented itself that afternoon. Mallory recognized the signs that his attention would be occupied by that puzzle for some time. She knew she'd probably have to remind him to eat. If she had to, she'd order from room service and feed it to him personally.

"What do you usually do in the evenings when you're here?" she asked him when they entered the sitting room of their suite.

Still distracted, Elliott shrugged as he tugged off his tie. "I usually spend the evening going over my notes, drawing up proposals to present to the group the next morning. I think I may have an idea on that distribution problem that had us all stumped this afternoon, but I'll have to think about it to make sure I haven't overlooked anything."

Mallory nodded, resigning herself to an evening of work and maybe a cable movie in her room. It didn't seem like a good time to bring up the subject of their relationship. "I'll type up my notes after I've changed.

What about dinner? Want me to order something from room service?"

"Mmm?" He looked around at her then, his brows drawn into a frown. "Oh, dinner. We'll order something later."

Much later and she'd be ready to start chewing on the furniture, Mallory thought grimly, but she decided she could wait an hour or so. After that she was ordering, whether Elliott was ready or not. "Fine."

He was already moving toward the open door to his bedroom where his portable computer waited for him. "Get those notes typed for me as quickly as you can," he tossed over his shoulder.

"Yes, sir," she drawled, knowing he didn't even hear her. Sighing gustily and reflecting on Joan's warnings about becoming involved with men like theirs, she headed for her own room where she changed into a comfortable lime-green sweat suit before turning on her typewriter.

She was almost finished transcribing the notes when Elliott cleared his throat from the doorway to get her attention. "I'm almost done, Elliott. Just another—" Her words died away as she looked up and spotted him.

Dressed in brief black swim trunks and a black-and-white striped T-shirt, a towel draped around his neck, Elliott leaned against the doorjamb, smiling at her. "Want to go for a swim?"

"A swim?" she repeated blankly. "But I haven't finished—"

He shook his head. "That can wait. You deserve a break. We both do. There's a pool downstairs. You did bring a bathing suit, didn't you?"

"Yes."

"Then put it on and let's go. I'll be waiting out here for you," he ordered, nodding toward the sitting room. "Impatiently," he added with another smile.

Smiling herself now, Mallory snapped off the typewriter and gave him a salute. "Yes, sir. Be just a minute, sir."

"Now that's the way I like you to respond to my instructions," Elliott approved, stepping back and closing her door between them.

Laughing at his teasing, and wondering if she would ever learn to predict his next move, Mallory hurried into her emerald green one-piece suit, topping it with a short terry wrap and sliding her feet into sandals.

Since it was dinnertime for most of the hotel guests, the pool was deserted, to Mallory's secret delight. Elliott stripped out of his shirt, kicked off his slip-on canvas shoes and dived in. Clearing her throat of the familiar lump that had formed at the sight of him so briefly clad, Mallory took her time shedding her own coverup. And then she walked down the steps into the shallow end of the pool, where she spent the next few minutes enjoying the silky feel of the cool water against her skin, splashing it onto her face and throat as Elliott swam a few laps, then went beneath the surface.

"You look gorgeous, you know," he said matter-of-factly, surfacing suddenly beside her.

She laughed, flushing a bit. "I'm wet," she pointed out.

"Mmm. I like you wet. And I like that bathing suit." Moving backward, he held out his hand to her. "Come swim with me."

She grimaced. "Um—Elliott?"

"Yeah?"

"I can't swim."

He stumbled, then caught himself, standing in chest-deep water to stare at her. "What?"

"I can't swim," she repeated defensively. "I never learned."

His grin seemed to spread from ear to ear. "No kidding."

"I don't see any reason for you to be quite so pleased about it," she grumbled. "Unless you're planning to drown me."

"I'm just finding it hard to believe that the so-competent Ms Littlefield doesn't know how to do something. Something *I* happen to do very well, I might add."

"You know perfectly well that there are many things you can do that I can't. And this is one of them. I can't swim."

His grin took on a slightly devilish tilt. "Lesson time," he announced succinctly.

She eyed him warily. "I beg your pardon?"

"Lesson time," he repeated. "Only now *I* get to be the teacher. I think I'm going to enjoy it."

She backed up as he advanced on her. "Now, Elliott, I'm not so sure this is a good idea."

"Right. That's what I said about the driving and dancing lessons, remember? Come on, Mallory, don't you want to fit into the real world?" he asked with mock astonishment. "Don't you want people to know you're independent and capable in the water as well as on solid ground?" He snagged her wrist as he spoke, pulling her gently toward him.

"You *are* going to drown me, aren't you?" she wailed.

He dropped a kiss on her water-beaded lips. "Oh, no, sweetheart. I have no intention of allowing any harm to befall this beautiful body. Now, come on, let me teach you to swim. It's the least I can do after all the free lessons you gave me."

She wasn't at all sure that she had a chance of learning to swim when she could hardly stand upright—and it hadn't even been a full-fledged kiss, she thought. But there was no way she could resist that particular smile. "Okay, Elliott," she said with a brave tilt of her chin. "Teach me to swim."

"That's my Mallory," he murmured approvingly, making her sink even lower into the water at his low, intimate tone. She was *definitely* going to drown, she thought, but at that moment she couldn't even bring herself to care. Not as long as Elliott was looking at her in just that way.

Perhaps Mallory wasn't quite as adept a pupil as Elliott had been. Or maybe the problem was that it was very hard for her to concentrate when Elliott stayed so close to her, barely dressed, his wet skin glistening invitingly, his eyes sweeping her body much too intimately to ignore. She almost drowned both of them before she finally managed to take a few successful strokes.

Laughing, Elliott caught her when she whooped her jubilation at her accomplishment and promptly sank. "You okay?" he asked when he tugged her to the surface, sputtering from the mouthful of water she'd swallowed.

"Did you see me, Elliott?" she asked, clinging to him to keep from going under again—the water came to his neck and was just over the top of her head. "I swam!"

"I saw you and you were great," he assured her. "But next time, maybe you'd better swim toward the shallow end. Didn't you know you were getting over your head?"

Suddenly she wasn't laughing. Her hands sliding slowly around his neck, she looked deep into his darkening eyes. "I think I was in over my head the day you walked into that employment agency," she told him in quiet candor.

He pulled her closer, until their wet, nearly bare bodies were pressed full-length, letting her know that their laughing water play had not dampened his need for her. "Mallory," he murmured, lowering his mouth to hers.

She was barely aware that she'd wrapped her legs around his hips as she tilted her head back to deepen the kiss. Her arms tightened around his neck, the fingers of one hand sliding into his wet hair to hold his mouth more firmly to hers. The slow undulation of her torso against his rigid arousal was purely instinctive.

A groan ripped its way from his chest, escaping between their clinging lips. His hand fell to her derriere, holding her hard against him. "God, I want you," he growled, still without pulling his mouth from hers.

"I know," she answered huskily, wriggling against him again.

His fingers tightened on her rounded flesh, holding her still. "You're going to get us arrested. Much more of that, and I'll take you right here in the pool."

"I want you, too, Elliott. Did I tell you?" she whispered, ignoring his warning. She nibbled at his lips, closing her eyes to savor the sheer bliss of touching him, being so very close to him, not even caring where they were. "I want you so much."

He moaned something incoherent and took her lips with a sudden savagery that made her mind shut down altogether. All she could do was hold on as he plundered the depths of her mouth without mercy, his tongue tangling with hers, conquering it, making it his. Her body throbbed almost painfully, fiercely aching for his possession, quivering with the need to take him so deeply inside her that he'd never want to be apart from her again.

"Mallory," he muttered, tearing his mouth from hers with a gasp. "Sweetheart, we have to stop."

She murmured a protest and sought his mouth again.

Pulling in a deep, unsteady breath, he held her off. "Let's go to our rooms."

She sighed deeply and opened her eyes. "What?"

"Our rooms," he repeated, beginning to smile, though the smile was decidedly shaky. "Private rooms—with locks on the doors—and beds."

Beds. The magic word. Mallory nodded emphatically, her wet ponytail bobbing with the movement. "Yes, let's go to our rooms."

Towing her into shallow water, Elliott turned with her toward the steps, only to stop in surprise when they both spotted Petra standing at the side of the pool, watching them with apparent interest.

Mallory flushed deeply at what the other woman must have seen, but Elliott didn't seem the least disconcerted. "Oh, hi, Petra. Were you looking for me?"

"Marcus is looking for you," she replied. "I was on my way to my room when I spotted you."

"Thanks. I'll call Marcus from my room." Elliott pulled himself out of the pool, unobtrusively wrapping his towel around his waist. Following closely, Mallory knew that Petra was as aware as Mallory of the reason Elliott chose to cover up with the towel rather than dry off. Pulling on his shirt and stepping into his shoes, Elliott turned to Mallory, who was just slipping into her wrap. "Ready?"

"I'll have to buckle my sandals. Why don't you go on and call Dr. Rosenzweig. I'll meet you in the suite."

He nodded. "Fine." He smiled briefly at Petra. "See you tomorrow."

"Yes, of course."

Mallory was rather surprised when Petra lingered after Elliott left them. Sitting on a poolside chair as she buckled her sandals, she tried to think of something to say to Elliott's former lover.

Petra took the decision out of her hands by speaking first. "I wanted to tell you how pleased I am about you and Elliott. He looks happier than I've ever seen him," she said without preamble.

Startled, Mallory pushed her hair back and looked up. "You really mean that, don't you?" she asked, noting the sincerity in Petra's expression.

Petra nodded briskly. "Yes. I do. I know Elliott has told you that he and I were once—involved, but I don't want you to feel threatened by that. The relationship was wrong for both of us and has been over for some time. I sensed this morning that you weren't quite comfortable with me, and I want you to know that I hope you'll be able to overcome that. We'll be seeing quite a bit of each other in the future, and I'd like for us to be friends."

Responding positively to Petra's plain speaking, Mallory rose to her feet and smiled. "I'd like that, too, Dr. Jantzen."

"Petra."

"Petra," Mallory repeated.

"You probably think it's odd of me to approach you this way."

Mallory laughed quietly. "No, not at all. I'm used to Elliott's directness. It's very refreshing, actually."

"Yes, well, neither of us is the type to waste time with prevarications when frankness is called for. I'm glad that you are able to deal with that. My own fiancé has learned to accept the way I am, but it hasn't always been easy for him."

"Your fiancé? You're engaged?"

Petra nodded again, her cheeks going uncharacteristically pink. "Yes. It's very recent. His name is Richard and he's—well, he makes me very happy."

"That's wonderful news," Mallory assured her warmly. "What does he do? Let me guess—a scientist, right? Or a professor."

Petra gave a rueful smile. "He's an insurance salesman. A very successful one, actually."

"An insurance salesman," Mallory repeated, struggling not to smile.

"Yes." Her expression telling that she knew how amused Mallory must be by the confession, Petra pushed her glasses higher on her straight nose. "He's outgoing, witty, charming. He makes me laugh, and he dares me to try things that I never considered attempting before. Last month we went backpacking into the mountains—last weekend he started teaching me to water-ski. He thinks I'm much too serious and introverted, but for some reason he loves me, and he wants to marry me."

"And you love him," Mallory observed confidently.

Her flush deepening prettily, Petra smiled. "Yes."

"Then you're very lucky,"

"So is Elliott," Petra said softly. "He has you."

Mallory knew right then that she and Petra would be friends, despite the past. The past no longer mattered; only the future. And her future was Elliott.

She and Petra parted warmly, then Mallory headed impatiently for the suite where her future waited for her, more determined than ever to make her relationship with Elliott work. Determined to convince him that no one could ever love him more than she did, that he needed her in his life as badly as she needed him in hers. That she no longer felt threatened by the intellectual side of him, because she had finally acknowledged that she had her own valuable contributions to make to his life.

And someday, maybe, he could learn to love her as much as she loved him.

12

ELLIOTT WAS ON THE PHONE, talking to Dr. Rosenzweig, when Mallory crossed the sitting room of their suite toward her own room. He grimaced ruefully at her, indicating that he might be a while longer. Still bemused by her conversation with Petra, she headed for the shower in her bathroom. As she washed the chlorine from her hair, she thought about what Petra had said, the happiness the other woman seemed to have found in her relationship with her fiancé. And then she thought about the time she'd spent with Elliott—the laughter, the passion, the confidences shared.

She couldn't give him up, she thought, suddenly fierce in her determination to keep this man in her life. She loved him as she'd never loved anyone before; she needed him with a desperation that had long since ceased to surprise her. And she could make him happy.

Her chin lifted, she stepped out of the shower, wrapped herself in an oversized towel and turned on her hair dryer, trying to decide how best to approach Elliott as she blew her hair dry to lie in soft coppery waves on her bare shoulders. She'd had his full concentration in the pool, but there was always the possibility, of course, that the telephone conversation with Dr. Rosenzweig had reclaimed his attention to the problems assigned to Option Forum. As she'd decided earlier, she didn't want to talk about their relationship unless she had his full attention.

Smiling a bit at the reflection in the mirror in front of her, she wondered if staging a grand seduction would make him notice her. Too bad she hadn't thought to bring her sexiest black teddy.

But then again, she mused, she *had* brought the midnight blue nightgown that he hadn't seemed able to resist in Chicago. Perhaps she'd finish typing his notes and then wear that to deliver them. And if that didn't work, she could always try tying him to a chair and shouting into his face.

Still planning her strategy, she stepped into her bedroom, only to realize that matters had already been taken out of her hands.

Wearing only a thigh-length white terry robe, his hair damp from his own quick shower, Elliott lounged on her bed, his long legs stretched comfortably in front of him. His eyes made an intimate survey of the skin her towel left bare. His hand lifted. "Come here," he urged, his voice husky.

The desire he'd roused in the swimming pool returned full force, immediately. Mallory took two eager steps toward the bed before stopping with a groan, a quick surge of panic paralyzing her where she stood. "I can't," she whispered.

His hand dropped. Swinging his legs to the side of the bed, Elliott looked at her with intense, narrowed eyes. "What's wrong? Did Petra say anything that bothered you?"

"No. This has nothing to do with Petra," she assured him flatly. "It has to do with you."

He let out a long, deep breath, the sound one of defeat. "You still have doubts. You're still not sure of what you feel for me."

"No. You're wrong. I know exactly what I feel for you," she told him with admirable composure, considering that her hands were trembling violently at her sides. "But I couldn't bear it if we made love again on an out-of-town interlude, only to have you shut me out when we return to the reality of home. I was devastated when you did that to me last time. I won't let you do it to me again."

Almost before she'd realized he'd moved, he was standing in front of her, his fingers gripping her shoulders. "Tell me," he ordered and she couldn't have missed the urgency in his voice. "Tell me how you feel about me."

She drew a deep breath for courage. "I love you. I think I have from the first, no matter how unwise I—"

She couldn't finish. His mouth effectively blocked any further words. Holding her as if he were afraid she'd vanish if he loosened his grasp, he kissed her until she quivered helplessly in his arms, knowing she wouldn't be able to stand on her own if he released her. The kiss lasted for an eternity and when it ended she pulled his mouth back to hers and kissed him with equal thoroughness.

She wasn't sure whose knees gave out first; they fell onto the bed still locked together, her towel lying unmissed on the floor where they'd stood.

"Tell me again," he demanded, his lips moving against hers, his hands sweeping the bare curves beneath him.

"I love you, Elliott. I love you so much." Her own fingers were busy with the loosely knotted belt of his robe.

"I love you," he repeated. "Oh, God, Mallory, how I love you." And, unable to bear even that brief separation, he brought his mouth down once more on hers.

Pulling his robe apart so that they were lying skin-to-skin, Mallory moved her lips over his face, pressing heated, loving kisses everywhere she paused. He loved her! Tears rolled down her face even as she laughed breathlessly in joyous triumph. Elliott loved her!

His mouth at her throat, Elliott cupped her right breast in his palm, his fingers tugging her nipple into a hard, straining peak. "We have to talk," he muttered, moving lower to kiss the ridge of her collarbone. "I have to tell you—I want to ask you to—"

His words ended in a gasp as she arched upward beneath him. And then words, questions were forgotten.

Their loving was hot, urgent, almost primitive. There was no past, no outside world, no thought of anyone or anything but each other and what they'd found together. The words they murmured were broken, nearly incoherent, but neither had trouble understanding the other. They rolled across the bed, flowing feverishly from one position to another, their movements becoming faster, more furious until finally they cried out together as spasms of release reclaimed them simultaneously.

And still it wasn't enough. Resting only for a moment, they began again. Touching, stroking, experimenting, murmuring encouragement and pleasure, repeatedly declaring their love in words and actions until, exhausted and more sated then either remembered being before, they fell back against the pillows, still holding each other as closely as possible.

Another lifetime later, Elliott finally stirred, sighed and announced in a wry, weary voice, "I think I need an ambulance."

Her cheek snuggled cozily into his shoulder, Mallory giggled. "Someone else will have to call one. I couldn't even push the buttons on the phone."

"I love you, Mallory."

As many times as he'd told her during their love-making, the words still had the power to stun her. She lifted her head to look at him, one hand going to touch his cheek as he smiled back at her. "You're sure, Elliott? You're absolutely sure? I couldn't bear it if you changed your mind."

"I won't change my mind," he promised, his voice deep. "I've never said those words to anyone outside my family. I wasn't even sure I could love a woman the way I love you. I want to share every morning, every night with you—for the rest of my life. I want you to marry me, work with me, have children with me, grow old with me. Will you?"

"Yes."

His eyes flared with emotion. "So quickly? You don't even want to think about it? I won't be the easiest man to live with, you know."

"You're the man I love," she answered gently, holding his gaze with her tender one. "There's no one I'd rather live with." She touched her mouth to his, softly, adoringly. "I love you, Elliott. I promise I'll make you happy."

"You do make me happy," he answered unsteadily, bringing her face back down to his shoulder and hugging her fervently. "I've never been so happy."

She hated to bring it up, but it was still there, haunting her, refusing to let her go. Watching her fingers as they idly stroked his chest, she asked tentatively, "Elliott, about that night in Chicago. Why did you turn so cold the next morning? What did I do to make you pull back so abruptly?"

"Oh, sweetheart, it wasn't you," he answered regretfully. "You did nothing wrong, nothing at all. I woke up that morning and realized that I'd fallen deeply, permanently in love with you, and it scared me witless. I didn't know what to do, how to tell you, whether you'd want to know. All that time I was accusing my family of believing me incapable of dealing with the real world—it turned out I was equally guilty of believing the same thing. I didn't think I had anything to offer you. I was afraid that I couldn't make you happy, that you'd change your mind about me, the way you did with—"

Frowning, she lifted her head again when he broke off. "The way I did with—?" she prompted.

"With that other man you once loved," he continued reluctantly. "The other man you worked for."

Mallory grimaced. "I *was* pretty adamant about not wanting another disastrous affair with my employer, wasn't I? I can see why you'd wonder if I was repeating an earlier mistake."

Taking a deep breath, she very calmly, without emotion, told him exactly what had happened between herself and Larry. "I thought I loved him," she finished quietly. "I knew almost immediately after we broke up that I had deluded myself. I wouldn't have gotten over him as easily as I did had I actually been in love with him. I would never had gotten over you. Never."

He relaxed measurably. "Were you afraid I would treat you as badly as he had?" he chided. "Use you and then leave you for someone I considered more suitable? Couldn't you tell I wasn't like that?"

"I couldn't help worrying about it," she admitted. "Both of us know that I'm not your intellectual equal— nor your social equal, for that matter. It had happened once. How could I be sure that it wouldn't happen again?"

"Mallory, you darling idiot. I don't want to compare IQ points or bank balances with the woman I love. Don't you know that you're everything I could ever need? You're bright, witty, warm, adorably optimistic, enchantingly willful. I never know what to expect from you next and yet I've thoroughly enjoyed anticipating your next surprise. You make me laugh, you make me ache, you make me crazy sometimes. And I'll never get enough of you."

Rapidly blinking back tears, she managed a watery smile. "I think I began to realize that you weren't comparing me to your academic associates after I met Petra. She's so beautiful, so brilliant, so poised, and yet as soon as I saw the two of you together, I knew you'd never be happy with her. She's very nice, by the way. I think she and I can be friends."

"I'm glad," he said simply.

"She's in love, too. She's going to be married," Mallory confided.

Elliott lifted a curious eyebrow. "Is she? I didn't know."

"Mmm. He's an insurance salesman. He's teaching her water-skiing and backpacking. I think he's decided she needs to learn a few ordinary, normal-people activities," she added gravely.

Elliott chuckled. "Imagine that."

"Yes. Imagine that." Mallory was quiet for a moment, then stirred restlessly. "Elliott?"

"Mmm?"

"I'm starving."

He grinned. "I did promise to feed you later, didn't I?"

"Yes, you did."

"How about a steak, baked potato and salad, with champagne to celebrate our engagement?"

Her stomach clenched in anticipation. "That sounds wonderful," she breathed.

He laughed at her enthusiasm. "Think you could manage to push the buttons on the phone now? We'll order from room service so we don't have to go to all that trouble of getting dressed to eat."

"And getting undressed afterward," she teased, her fingertips sliding wantonly down his stomach.

He trapped her wrist in his hand. "Unless you want to put us both in the hospital from malnourishment and exhaustion, you'd better behave and call room service."

She tilted her head for a moment as if considering her options, then gave him a bright, challenging smile. "Think you'll be—um—up to it after you've eaten?"

His grin answered her dare. "I think you're the one who'd better get plenty of protein."

"Is that right?"

"That's right," he confirmed with teasing arrogance.

"I believe I've mentioned before that I have created a monster."

"So you have. And I believe that I've told you before that you're quite right."

"What about your work? Your proposal for tomorrow?"

"I'll finish it while we wait for our dinner. Quickly." He caught her hand in his, bringing her knuckles to his lips as he grew suddenly serious. "My work will always be important to me, Mallory, but I think you'll be able to keep me from becoming too immersed in it. Never doubt that you are more important to me than anything else. Anything. I love you."

"I love you, too." Swallowing a lump in her throat, Mallory smiled tremulously and reclaimed her hand. "I'll call room service. You go turn on your computer."

Epilogue

MALLORY LICKED the back of the stamp, slapped it in the upper right-hand corner of the envelope and added the letter to the pile of twenty identical envelopes lying on the dining room table in front of her. Stretching wearily, she grimaced at the gummy taste in her mouth, telling herself for the countless time that she and Elliott were going to have to invest in a postage machine. Checking her watch, she noted it was past ten—and Elliott was still downstairs in his office, immersed in the complexities of a new software package he'd been working on for months. Unless she managed to drag him away from his computer, she knew he could well be in his office all night.

She'd been working in the dining room so that she'd be able to hear any cries coming from the small bedroom closest to the one she shared with her husband. Envelopes tucked under one arm, she stopped by that room on her way to the stairs. Tiptoeing into the dimly lighted room, she paused by the Jenny Lind baby bed, smiling at the tiny baby sleeping within it.

Four-month-old Laurie preferred sleeping on her stomach, diapered bottom stuck high in the air. Assured that her daughter was out for the night, Mallory lightly stroked her soft copper curls before turning to slip back out of the room.

Downstairs she dropped her correspondence on the desk in her office before squaring her shoulders and facing the closed door to Elliott's office, still affectionately referred to by the two of them as "the pit."

Just as she'd expected, she found him huddled over his keyboard, muttering to himself. "Elliott?"

"Mmmph," he mumbled without taking his eyes from the glowing monitor.

"Elliott, it's late and you have an early class in the morning," she continued firmly, knowing as she spoke that she might as well have been addressing the computer. "Come to bed now."

"Yes, sweetheart. Just a minute." His fingers flew over the keyboard and the symbols on the monitor flashed furiously. "That's not *right*," he grumbled in frustration, glaring at the screen.

"Elliott, darling. Your underwear is on fire. You're endangering an important part of your anatomy," she told him sweetly, standing behind him with her arms crossed over her chest, one foot tapping silently on the carpet.

He never even blinked as he cleared the screen and punched in a new series of commands. "Thanks, honey. I'll take care of it."

This was going to take drastic measures. It wouldn't be the first time she'd had to get creative during their two very happy years of marriage; she was quite sure it wouldn't be the last. Thoughtfully chewing her lower lip, she began to loosen the buttons at the right wrist of her black silk blouse. "Elliott, darling. You can work on this tomorrow."

"Fine." He didn't look up, not even when the silk blouse was draped provocatively over his shoulder. He never even noticed it lying there.

"You're going to be too tired to concentrate on your other work if you don't get some rest tonight."

"Mmm-hmm." Her gray flannel slacks fell unnoticed at his feet.

"Are you coming to bed now?"

"Mmm."

Mallory smiled and reached for the hem of her camisole.

Some distant part of his mind knew she was there, that she wanted his attention. One more moment, Elliott thought vaguely, and he'd turn to Mallory. If only he could figure out how to get past this one minor glitch in his program. Maybe if he tried another...

He frowned as something fell over the monitor, obscuring the screen. Something dark. Impatiently, he reached out to brush it away. Prepared to toss it aside, he paused as his fingers tangled in soft fabric. Soft, silky, black fabric. Trimmed in lace. Scented with the lightly floral fragrance that Mallory always wore.

Mallory.

Tearing his bemused gaze away from the scrap of fabric in his hand, he turned his head. His breath jammed in his throat.

She wore nothing but a minuscule triangle of black silk and lace low on her slender hips. Her glossy red hair fell around her bare shoulders, begging him to bury his hands in it. And she was smiling at him with so much love that it made his chest ache.

"You are so very beautiful," he murmured, work forgotten.

Her smile deepened. "More beautiful than your computer?"

"More beautiful than anything." He surged to his feet, reaching for her."

"Don't forget to store your work," she reminded him.

He did so impatiently, then turned off the computer, whirled swiftly and gathered her into his arms, swinging her high against his chest. "Did I hear you say something about bed, Mrs. Fraser?"

Laughing, she wrapped her arms around his neck. "Elliott, you idiot, put me down. You can't carry me all the way upstairs."

He grinned. "Want to bet?"

She stopped protesting and snuggled into his shoulder in a gesture of trust that moved him as deeply as her smile had only moments earlier. He carried her up the stairs without the least bit of difficulty. He paused for a moment at the door to the nursery. "Laurie?"

"Laurie is fine," she assured him.

He smiled and moved on, crossing their bedroom in four long strides, to tumble to the bed with her beneath him.

"All right, I'm impressed," she admitted, hands locked behind his head. "You're in wonderful shape, Dr. Fraser."

"I'm rather fond of your shape as well," he returned, his hands thoroughly exploring that shape.

Her fingers went to the buttons of his shirt. "You're not annoyed with me?"

His lips pressed to the upper curve of one small, perfect breast, he spoke against her skin. "Now why should I be annoyed with you?"

"For interrupting your work."

Fingertips slipping beneath the elastic band of her bikini panties, he chuckled quietly. "Hardly. Didn't I once tell you that I was sure you'd find ways to distract me when I tended to become too immersed in a project?"

"Lucky for me I know your weaknesses," she murmured with a low laugh, hands still busy with the fastenings of his clothing. "You're really not all that hard to distract, my darling husband."

"I'd have to be blind and neutered not to be distracted by you standing in front of me wearing nothing but these sexy panties, Mrs. Fraser. I like your style."

She grew abruptly serious. "Oh, Elliott, I do love you."

His eyes darkened, his voice deepening as he spoke tenderly. "And I love you. You've given me so much during the past two years. A beautiful daughter, a happy home, love, passion, laughter. I never realized how empty my life was when all I had was my work— not until I compared it to what I've found with you. God knows I haven't always been easy for you to live with, either."

Dropping his shirt to the floor beside the bed, she stared fiercely up at him. "Don't you ever doubt that our marriage has made me happier than I've ever been before, Elliott Fraser. You've been a wonderful husband and I couldn't ask for a more loving father for our child. There hasn't been a day in the past two years that I haven't been grateful that you walked into that employment agency and swept me into your life. I love you. I always will."

He kissed her deeply, almost gratefully, then reached impatiently to remove the remainder of his clothing.

And then he proceeded to demonstrate just how deeply he loved her, how thoroughly she aroused him even after two years of intimacy. How much he would always want her, no matter how many years they would have together.

Her eyes closing in blissful enjoyment, Mallory gave herself up to the hands of her own beloved genius, confident that she'd been lucky enough to find the perfect place for herself. Sending silent thanks to that imaginary drummer she'd been following so long, for leading her to Elliott, she concentrated on giving her husband as much pleasure as he was giving her, smiling her contentment when he left her in no doubt of her success.

HARLEQUIN Temptation

COMING NEXT MONTH

SWEEPSTAKES RULES & REGULATIONS

NO PURCHASE NECESSARY TO ENTER OR RECEIVE A PRIZE

1. To enter and join the Reader Service, check off the ''YES'' box on your Sweepstakes Entry Form and return to Harlequin Reader Service. If you do not wish to join the Reader Service but wish to enter the Sweepstakes only, check off the ''NO'' box on your Sweepstakes Entry Form. Incomplete and/or inaccurate entries are ineligible for that section or sections(s) of prizes. Not responsible for mutilated or unreadable entries or inadvertent printing errors. Mechanically reproduced entries are null and void. Be sure to also qualify for the Bonus Sweepstakes. See rule #3 on how to enter.

2. Either way, your unique Sweepstakes number will be compared against the list of winning numbers generated at random by the computer. In the event that all prizes are not claimed, random drawings will be held from all entries received from all presentations to award all unclaimed prizes. All cash prizes are payable in U.S. funds. This is in addition to any free, surprise or mystery gifts that might be offered. The following prizes are offered:* Grand Prize (1) $1,000,000 Annuity; First Prize (1) $35,000; Second Prize (1) $10,000; Third Prize (3) $5,000; Fourth Prize (10) $1,000; Fifth Prize (25) $500; Sixth Prize (5,000) $5.

   * This Sweepstakes contains a Grand Prize offering of a $1,000,000 annuity. Winner may elect to receive $25,000 a year for 40 years without interest; totalling $1,000,000 or $350,000 in one cash payment. Entrants may cancel Reader Service at any time without cost or obligation to buy.

3. Extra Bonus Prize: This presentation offers two extra bonus prizes valued at $30,000 each to be awarded in a random drawing from all entries received. To qualify, scratch off the silver on your Lucky Keys. If the registration numbers match, you are eligible for the prize offering.

4. Versions of this Sweepstakes with different graphics will be offered in other mailings or at retail outlets by Torstar Corp. and its affiliates. This promotion is being conducted under the supervision of Marden-Kane, Inc., an independent judging organization. By entering this Sweepstakes, each entrant accepts and agrees to be bound by these rules and the decisions of the judges, which shall be final and binding. Odds of winning in the random drawing are dependent upon the total number of entries received. Taxes, if any, are the sole responsibility of the winners. Prizes are nontransferable. All entries must be received by March 31, 1990. The drawing will take place on or about April 30, 1990 at the offices of Marden-Kane, Inc., Lake Success, N.Y.

5. This offer is open to residents of the U.S., United Kingdom and Canada, 18 years or older, except employees of Torstar Corp., its affiliates, subsidiaries, Marden-Kane and all other agencies and persons connected with conducting this Sweepstakes. All Federal, State and local laws apply. Void wherever prohibited or restricted by law.

6. Winners will be notified by mail and may be required to execute an affidavit of eligibility and release, which must be returned within 14 days after notification. Canadian winners will be required to answer a skill-testing question. Winners consent to the use of their name, photograph and/or likeness for advertising and publicity in conjunction with this or similar promotions, without additional compensation.

7. For a list of our most current major prize winners, send a stamped, self-addressed envelope to: Winners List, c/o Marden-Kane, Inc., P.O. Box 701, Sayreville, N.J. 08871.

If Sweepstakes entry form is missing, please print your name and address on a 3″ × 5″ piece of plain paper and send to:

In the U.S.	In Canada
Sweepstakes Entry	Sweepstakes Entry
901 Fuhrmann Blvd.	P.O. Box 609
P.O. Box 1867	Fort Erie, Ontario
Buffalo, NY 14269-1867	L2A 5X3